PIPER HUGULEY

12 Days of *Christmas*
MAIL ORDER BRIDES

The Swan
The Seventh Day

D0563200

The Swan
The Twelve Days of Christmas Mail-Order Brides
The Seventh Day

by
Piper Huguley

Twelve Days of Christmas Mail-Order Brides
The Swan: The Seventh Day
by Piper Huguley

© 2017 Piper Huguley

All rights reserved. No part of this book may be reproduced in any form, except for brief quotations in printed reviews, without permission in writing from the publisher. All characters are fictional. Any resemblances to actual people or livestock are purely coincidental.

Cover design by Erin Dameron-Hill and EDH Creations

License Note

This e-book is licensed for your personal enjoyment only. This e-book may not be re-sold or given away to other people. If you would like to share this book with another person, please purchase an additional copy for each recipient. If you're reading this book and did not purchase it, or it was not purchased for your use only, then please return and purchase your own copy. Thank you for respecting the hard work of this author.

ACKNOWLEDGEMENTS

Sandra Belle Calhoune, Vanessa Riley and Julie Hilton Steele—my three writing friends who continue to hold me up. Thank you.

DEDICATION

This one is for my tall, elegant sister—Heather Lynn Harris, always a lovely swan--never a cygnet.

"But what did he see in the clear stream below? His own image; no longer a dark, gray bird, ugly and disagreeable to look at, but a graceful and beautiful [cob] swan. To be born in a duck's nest, in a farmyard, is of no consequence to a bird, if it is hatched from a swan's egg."
Hans Christian Andersen.
The Ugly Duckling (Illustrated)

CHAPTER ONE
December 23, 1876

This morning, Liam Fulton would not have believed that in the afternoon he would be in the fresh-smelling piney woods of Noelle looking for a Christmas tree to welcome the mail-order brides. He wasn't one of the grooms. Yet, here he was. The proposition reminded him of his childhood. How beautiful the tree would look when they affixed small candles to the branches—once he was able to find them in his mess of a dry goods store. The memory of it all warmed him inside. He had to admit, it felt good to do something charitable for the other men in Noelle who were getting themselves gussied up for the arrival of their brides. Christmas was a special time, and he didn't mind helping others have a special time to get this community settled.

Tom, one of the miners, nudged him as they walked through the woods. "You didn't want one of the brides, Liam?"

"Good things come to those who wait." Liam intoned to his friend who liked to play checkers at his dry goods store.

Orvis Stovall, another miner, spoke. "I agree. I think they'll have all the desperate ones in this first group. The next group, that one will have the real beauties."

Liam frowned against the falling snow. "That's not what I meant."

"Don't joke like that with this man," Tom said to Orvis. "He can get very defensive if you joke about the wrong thing."

Well, who liked to be misinterpreted? In reality, Liam felt sorry for the brides. Some of the men, one, that fool JD Jones was very disrespectful about everything he was going to do to his bride as soon as they got married. Some of the men laughed at his crude pantomimes and jokes, but Liam didn't join in.

Tom rubbed his hands against the cold. He needed a better coat but was too cheap to come into Liam's store. "Madam and her girls are here. It's good enough to blow off some energy with them. Liam likes that high yaller girl she got."

"Is it really necessary to talk of these matters in the open air?" Liam shouted over his shoulder at the others. Liam was not an outdoors man. He was a shopkeeper and before that, a sometimes schoolmaster and soldier in the Civil War. He was in the middle of studying for his oral law exams to become a lawyer. A lot of these fellows didn't understand his approach to things, but he didn't want to judge. Still, one thing he knew was that he would stand up to combat injustice if he saw it. His father had been a friend of John Brown and, like him, had spoken out against enslavement long before it was fashionable to do so. The streak to protect the weak was strong in him.

"Maybe you want to marry her."

Liam shook his head. "I would want better than that for her. Angelique is just a kid."

"Yet, you go to her."

A fury rose up in Liam, but he said nothing. He gripped the handle of his ax a bit tighter, wanting to take his anger out on chopping down a tree instead of this idiot miner who might be a better customer one day. His encounters with Angelique were none of anyone's business. "There. What about that one?"

"It's a little crooked."

"You can cut off the branches on that one side to even it out. Will it fit into the saloon?"

"I think so." Tom agreed.

Liam walked up to the fir tree and stripped off some of the lower branches to prepare it for chopping. It would surely look beautiful all decorated for the holidays.

He wanted a bride same as anyone. But when the time came, he would do his own choosing. William Cobb Fulton had always been his own man. He made his own rules. Noelle would settle just the same without him.

Turning to the tree instead of the insolent miner, he brought his ax down onto the wood with a hearty and satisfying "thwack."

December 24, 1876

When they all got off the train and were taken to sleighs driven by mules, Avis finally understood by the cold and the snow that they were in the mountains of Colorado. She sat in the row next to the young woman holding a goose and another woman holding a baby. Interesting company. Their mere variety appealed to her. She had never had a friend that was her own age. No one would ever accept her for who she really was. If these brides knew her, really knew her, the rejections would continue. She didn't need that.

7

The heavy weight of her tightly wound chignon pressed into her head and neck. It would be better if she kept far away from the other brides.

She clutched her Bible. It tended to keep people distant. Not this time though, Molly, the young woman holding the goose, peered over. "You're a believer, I see."

"Yes." Another lie. "I'm praying because I can't wait to meet my future husband."

"Who is he?" Kezia, the beautiful woman with the sweet baby girl, asked.

"John D. Jones. He's a miner."

One of the brides, Josefina, had deep olive colored skin and black silk ringlets that danced when she laughed. She had approached Avis back at Benevolent Lambs, reached out her hand and said, "Call me Fina."

Fina now said, "You got a miner? Bueno! I have the restaurant owner. We'll make our money feeding everyone. I'm looking forward to laying eyes on that Nacho. What do you think your man will be like?"

"Goodness." Avis wanted to say she hadn't given John D. Jones a moment's thought. He was old, like forty or something. He said something in his letter about wanting a family to hand his fortune off to and marrying a devout woman who would teach them to love the Lord.

She recalled what Mrs. Walters said to her. "That's why I matched you with him, Avis. I thought you would be perfect."

Foolishness. Nothing but foolishness. Where would some man twice as old as she get babies from with her? She shuddered but could see that Fina was waiting for her answer, as were all of the brides. They stopped what they were doing, all curious about her. "I don't know, " Avis answered quickly. "I guess we'll find out soon."

"We'll certainly be there soon." Fina smiled at her, but the smile didn't light up her face as the other smiles she had given did. Now that Fina could see Avis wasn't like her and wouldn't laugh or crack jokes like the other brides, she rejected Avis.

There were some bumps in the journey. Once, some of the brides had to dig the sleigh out of the snow and Avis helped. It kept her hands busy. She did her work and said nothing. She had done worse before. At one home, she was forced to pull a plow through the rocky New England soil like a mule. So digging out a wagon was nothing. That one named Maybelle did nothing, but Avis did her part. She wanted no thank yous. She really didn't care to speak to Maybelle at all.

Don't worry about her. Worry about what you came to do.

Still, the brides cheered when a young man came out with a team of mules to save them from further digging in the snow. It looked like everything was working out for them. The other brides all seemed glad to arrive. Avis felt glad for them. They deserved happiness.

Their excitement still didn't give her comforting feelings for what would happen...after. Would she finally be accepted in a real home somewhere? After confronting Betsey?

The man with the mules escorted the brides to a large building that read, The Golden Nugget. It was the town saloon, clearly. Avis had seen enough of those in her day. Still, each woman was treated as a piece of porcelain. But to Avis, this seemed silly. That wasn't her.

One man stood at the front of The Golden Nugget, waving his hat. He reached up and helped each one of the brides off of the first sleigh. A murmur went through the brides and finally reached her. "Avis," Mrs. Walters said, "That's John Jones. I recognize him from the description I was sent."

He wasn't very tall, she noticed and no matter how she tried to quench it, a bubble of disappointment rose within her. That was her husband? The murmur went back to where he was standing. Several of the brides indicated to him that she was Avis Smith.

When he reached into the sleigh for her, his look shifted to an all too familiar look of rejection. The nervousness in his face shifted to something hard. Something familiar.

"Good day," Avis said in her best pious lady voice.

The man's beady eyes shifted to the ground. "Hmmm, Yeah. Heh."

He dropped her hand as if she were a hot coal and ran away like something were after him, not helping the rest of them down. *What was wrong with him? Was he disappointed?*

More rejection. She should have been used to it, but it still rankled. Oh well, she was in Noelle now. She needed to figure out where Betsey Smith lived in this community.

When they all gathered in the large saloon, the brides stood in a group on one side and some of the men watched them. Including JD Jones. He didn't approach her, but stood to the side with his lip thrust out in a most unhappy gesture.

Mrs. Walters seemed preoccupied with the gentleman who had

introduced himself as Reverend Chase Hammond as they exited the wagons. She had a problem, and it looked as if Mrs. Walters had a problem too. Avis could see her waving her hands, talking loud, but not loud enough for them to hear.

In a few moments, Mrs. Walters came to them, her green eyes snapping with fight. "We are going to be taken to better quarters than this, fortunately. There will be no weddings until I'm assured that the quarters we were all promised really do exist."

"Come this way, ladies," Chase Hammond said in voice that rang false to Avis. Some reverend this town had.

CHAPTER TWO

Even though Liam had a lot to do on Christmas Eve, his curiosity got the better of him. He had prayed for JD's bride, and he wanted to see her and the arrival of the brides. The brides huddled at one end of the saloon. JD was being confronted by one of the women, who was well-dressed and very attractive, but clearly upset. What could be the problem?

Liam's gaze went to where JD Jones stood, pouting. He knew Jones was behind this in some way. He had drawn a short straw, and Liam bet he was at the bottom of this trouble. From the door of the saloon, he could smell the pitiful man above everything: the tree, the sweat of nervous men and the perfume of the frozen women. It tested his nerve that the town might fail because of that sawed-off, short, powder keg of a man, with his slicked-up hair which stunk of the bergamot he got at Liam's store. He used way too much, probably in hopes of covering up his putrid body odor.

It wasn't fair to the ladies to be cold and huddled together. He left his table to see if he could assist Chase Hammond, but he and the other woman had left, and the women were leaving with them. He was too late. "What's going on?" he asked Tom who had also come to The Golden Nugget to see the arrival.

Tom stood next to him, watching the attractive women depart back into the cold. What a rude and unpleasant arrival.

"JD says his bride is a daughter of Ham. He says he ain't gonna marry her and now..."

"Now what?" Liam asked. "I'm not surprised JD is the one trying to wriggle out of what he promised to do." The man owed him hundreds of dollars.

Liam stepped out into the cold outdoors and watched JD watching them go. A small group of miners joined them. The little man stomped on the wooden sidewalk. "What if we got buyer's remorse?"

"What?" Liam's brow furrowed. Which one of those poor women had been cursed with the burden of this infernal man?

JD whirled on him. "I said, what if we got the buyer's remorse? You know we saw what we got but don't want it?"

A murmur went through the crowd of men. Tom spoke up. "Well now,

JD. You drew your straw, signed on for this and paid for your lady to get here. Now she's here, and you don't want her?"

Liam shook his head. "We've got to show this town is getting settled with these twelve couples and you just can't—"

"I said I don't want her," The little man screamed like a child. "They ought to send her back."

Cries of "Why not?" echoed across the group.

The handful of men looked over to where JD pointed at the retreating back of one of the brides.

JD sputtered. "She's one of them mulatto womens. From down in New Orleans way."

"What are you talking about, JD?" One of the men shouted. "These brides come from Denver."

The little man shook his head back and forth; his stringy black hair slid from his pate. "You don't get what I'm saying. She's... she's colored."

The men murmured amongst themselves as JD spoke his accusation.

What difference did that make? Why should these women be so rudely received in Noelle? Liam couldn't take it anymore and started down the street after the retreating women. He was determined to get to the bottom of this. Disappointment surged through him. The men had thought there would be weddings today. They had even gathered some of the miners who played instruments together for music to be played for the weddings. Liam loved music. It was one of the reasons he came today, even though he wasn't a groom. And what of the tree? Should they move the tree?

They seemed to be going down to the cathouse. It was cold outside, but in short order he caught up with the women who had just reached La Maison. He stood at the edge of the group and went in with them as they were all admitted. He followed a young woman of Chinese descent who seemed hesitant to enter. He could understand why.

Liam approached Chase Hammond, but he couldn't get to him because he was almost knocked down by Sam Goodwin who ran out of the cathouse in the "altogether." Liam sighed. Just another day at La Maison du Chats. Some of the brides screamed at the sight of Goodwin's pallid hindquarters retreating into the dusk of the day. Well, they were Benevolent Lambs. He turned to help the reverend apologize at this turn of events. Their faces, swathed by hoods and covered with bonnets, contained degrees of upset. He opened his mouth, but then another man, who was even more naked than Sam

12

Goodwin, ran out into the cold. Many of the women covered their mouths to stop the stunned sounds from escaping. Many, except one. The one with the eyes, and the most beautiful woman he had ever seen, dared to look at him, unashamed and unafraid of who she was. She stood, proud like the Christmas tree he had cut down yesterday. There was no shock or startled scream from her. JD's bride.

He had prayed for the woman ever since JD had drawn a short straw. He wanted to come closer to the focus of his prayers. The women had started to take off their wraps, so he could see she had a black dress on — appropriate for the occasion of having to marry JD. She took off her bonnet and her dark brown eyes refocused on him with curiosity.

He could see her strength in her eyes and the way she held her elegant, long neck. She wasn't afraid of anyone in this room, and he admired her spirit.

Liam stepped to the other side of the room. "Is everything okay, ladies?"

Just as the words came from his mouth, two of the women fainted. He rushed to them, but several of the brides surrounded them both, blocking his view.

The woman stepped in next to him. "They'll be fine. It's been a long journey."

"We have food and coffee." Milly, the cathouse cook, stepped forward, eager to make a good show. Milly used her bulk to edge her way in to seeing after the brides who had fainted, but they were already coming around. "Pearl can show you to your rooms." She gestured toward blonde Pearl who was one of Madam's girls.

"Yes, please." One of the ladies peeled off towards the door, declaring, "So many awful things. Naked men and Avis is a Negro. Who could imagine? There shouldn't be any Negro people in Noelle. Negroes give me the creeps. They're bad luck."

Liam said a quick prayer for whomever would have to marry that one. He noticed the mean one had glared and gestured to the woman who was right next to him.

Turning to her, he took some time to appreciate her lovely face more closely. Her nose was freckled and something inside of him warmed at the sight. The freckles only increased her charm. "Are you all right? Do you need a glass of punch? Maybe a glass of our best spring water?"

Her brow furrowed, and in that long moment, Liam noticed the woman's lips. They were well shaped and full, but not like a Negro's full lip. He was having a hard time seeing it in her.

Suddenly the woman seemed to understand why he was appraising her so closely, and her full lips curled up and practically spat at him. "No. I don't need anything from any of you."

Well. He was just trying to be nice. "Fine then."

He retreated and saw JD Jones in the front of the cathouse raising up a fuss, as well as his usual stink. JD's bride had a lot of spice in her, that one. Wormy little JD needed a woman with a backbone and a lot of spice. *Happy marriage, JD Jones.*

Grandpa Gus came in, declaring to all in a loud voice that he had a bride to claim. Fortunately, Jack came in and helped settle his grandfather.

Liam looked back at the woman who had retreated to a chair all alone. Another woman, whom he guessed was the matchmaker of the brides, Mrs. Walters, came to the fascinating woman and spoke to her in low nurturing tones while patting the rejected bride on the shoulder. His heart pounded as Mrs. Walters said, "Mr. Jones," a time or two.

JD had rejected this woman for being a Negro? No longer as proud as it was before, the woman's face crumbled. Something inside of her seemed resigned.

Her hair. Sometimes it was there, but no. This woman's hair was smoothed back into shiny ebony glass and twisted and twirled in a heavy knot that rested on the back of her long, elegant neck. How much hair was coiled and twisted up in there? What did it look like cascading down her shoulders? She probably had enough hair for everyone in here. What would it be like to kiss her neck?

Liam shook his head from the improper thought and focused on a time when the men first started discussing this months ago. He tried to tell them something like this was a possibility. Sometimes women ran from things: husbands, previous children, lives as whores, all kinds of things they knew nothing of. Yet and still, the men of Noelle were willing to put the future of the town on the line to have women come in from Denver. It was no surprise that any of them should lie. The future lawyer in him worked his way back to their side of the room to hear what Mrs. Walters was saying.

He edged himself closer to the pair of women so he could better hear Mrs. Walter's low, well-modulated voice. The grooms had paid for their

14

brides to come part of the way on the train. Ahh, JD was out his money. Which was stupid because the fool paid for what he wanted. She was here now. A beautiful woman. A proud woman. A young woman. Angelique was a kid, but this woman was older than her by five or six years. Certainly at least ten years younger than his thirty-five, minimally.

Here he was, William C. Fulton, son of an important abolitionist couple who could not stand to see anyone suffer. The Negro people in this country had come here in chains. This beautiful woman was in a bind for sure. If JD didn't get his money back, what would happen to her? What would happen to Noelle?

He thought of Madam Bonheur somewhere in this cathouse. A hard-hearted business woman if there ever was one. She would have no compunctions about taking in someone who looked like this woman. He saw it all, because he had seen it all. This beautiful woman, no matter what her origin, faced the trajectory of a hard, difficult life with no way out. Just like Angelique. This woman didn't deserve that. None of them did. This woman, with the blood of survivors running in her veins, had risked it all, risked whatever she had to come out here into the unknown. That should be rewarded not punished.

Liam stood and went to Mrs. Walters. "Excuse me, I couldn't help but overhear. Are you still having a problem?"

Mrs. Walters straightened, but there was determination in her pose as she looked at him. "This matter doesn't concern you, sir."

"I know, but I want to help. I'm a lawyer."

The women stared at him as if he had lit up like the Christmas tree.

The full lips parted to speak, but her tone was different. "Why would you want to help a stranger? A colored one at that?"

"My folks worked on the Underground Railroad before the war. I fought on the Union side. Lots didn't know what the war was about, but I knew. It was always wrong to hold an entire race in bondage. That's what I fought for. So, I want to help."

"Her passage money. Her groom, Mr. Jones, wants to be paid back for her passage. We aren't going back to Denver right now. I don't have the money to—"

"I do. I'll pay him," Liam said. "That man has a whole tab with me. I'll cancel part of it."

Mrs. Walters put a hand to her throat. "That's very kind. Why on earth would you do such a thing? Who are you anyway?"

"William Cobb Fulton, ma'am. Folks call me Liam." He held out a hand to Mrs. Walters, and she shook it.

"Well, it looks as if you are an early Christmas present for our Avis here. This is Avis Smith. Thank you. We still have to worry about getting the marriages in for Noelle, but this is certainly a first step toward a resolution. I'll see if the Reverend and I can speak to Mr. Jones and tell him what has happened. Thank you again." She left them.

Liam turned to speak to her. "Avis. That's a pretty name."

The woman faced him, features arranged to have a hiss fit again. "She may not know why you did what you did, Mr. Fulton, but I do."

"You do?"

"All of that about working on the Underground Railroad. A cover story. You want a bed warmer."

"A bed what? No. You have it wrong."

"Well, I cannot let you pay my way. I won't be bought and sold."

He could see her point. Something inside of him wilted at how he had potentially dishonored her. "Well, I run the dry goods store here. You can work for me if you like," Liam nodded. "Yes, I think if you work at the store, you'll pay off the debt, and it will give you a chance to see more of the men here in Noelle. I'm sure one of them would be willing to marry you before the deadline. What do you say?"

A soft, warm glow broke out behind her freckles. "I'm sorry about the way I spoke to you earlier. I didn't mean to be mean."

"It's quite all right. It smells like Milly has some food cooking. Would you like something to eat after you see your living quarters?"

The glow on her face spread. "Yes, please." She stood as she looked him in the eyes. "Thank you, Mr. Fulton. I appreciate the help."

"Wonderful. I'll go tell Mrs. Walters about my offer and then I'll see how we can get you taken care of."

Liam moved to the door, and it occurred to him, as it often repeatedly did, that JD Jones was the biggest idiot in the world.

CHAPTER THREE

The sheriff in town had been recruited to get the working girls to leave the house for an abandoned saloon across the street. Supper had been postponed until they were nearly all evicted. Once supper was over, the brides relaxed in the parlor. Avis sought to use her time to be nice to the man who, in essence, had saved her hide. "You say you run a dry goods store?"

"Yes, you passed it on the way here. These ones who want to search for silver are finding nothing but quartz. It's pretty enough, but you have to crush it up to make it be something. I'm content making my loot selling things the miners need."

"That makes a lot of sense." They stood by the fireplace, talking to one another. Avis bit into a spice cookie laid out by the cathouse cook for dessert and enjoyed the warm spiciness of it. "Are you selling these? Because they are delicious."

"Milly made some special. She doesn't usually do that because Madam would—"

A hoarse female voice came screaming into the parlor making the brides jump. Avis didn't jump. The nose on the older woman looked very familiar. Could she be Betsey Smith?

"And here she is." Liam rolled his eyes. "She hasn't left yet."

Avis kept her gaze steady. Just as she did before JD humiliated her. "Who is she?"

"Madam Bonheur. The head, ummm, lady of this cathouse. She's not too thrilled at having to find a new place to conduct her business over the holidays." Avis watched him as he lowered his head and shook his long red locks.

It was never easy for her to make herself invisible when she had to. Avis always stuck out for one reason or another. But this man, Liam Fulton, was a shade taller than her so she enfolded herself into his shadow and ate more of the spicy goodness of the cookie as she watched. The time was near, and now she had to think carefully on what she would do to make things happen.

"I don't have to be 'appy. I still don't want zeese women in my house." The voice came right from her nostrils. The way everyone was wincing, it

17

was clear Madam's voice grated on everyone who listened to her. It was said that the men were happy to give her silver if she didn't speak, but Avis couldn't keep her eyes off the woman. She wore a fancy sparkly dress. She was short, not of medium height like Avis, but Avis knew from what some of the early keepers had told her that she got her height from her father. Madam's hair was piled on top of her head in a pompadour. Her white skin mottled with red as she told the Reverend off regarding his plan.

"Madame Bonheur, it will only be for a few days over the Christmas holidays. No one is coming to you on Christmas, I hope?" Chase Hammond swallowed.

"Zat is my best time! That is when the miners want a drink and the company of a female! You ruin it all for me."

The way she moved her hands... Avis noticed. Very familiar.

"What if we pay you something?"

The madam stilled. Now he was singing her tune. "I want it up front."

"Of course. I have to see what the town council is willing to pay."

"Bah. Always politicians trying to figure out where I fit in. Well, I pay taxes in this town like everyone else. I have a business like most. You wouldn't zink of kicking zem out of their business."

"The women have to be comfortable."

"They've been writing to their husbands. Don't they have homes for them?"

"That's not the way we operate." Genevieve Walters spoke quietly, "All of our brides are quality candidates."

Some men who came into the room guffawed at this response. Avis pulled back a little from the laughter until she noticed a young face next to Madam focused on her. Ahh.

Avis saw the blackness in Madam's companion as soon as she looked at her. Her skin tone was darker for one. "Who is she?" Avis asked Mr. Fulton. "She's looking at me mighty hard."

Liam looked back and forth between the two women, and then waved to the young girl. The young girl waved shyly at Mr. Fulton but stayed close to the raging madam. "That's Angelique."

"So, you know Angelique?" Why did it matter to Avis? She had only met this man a short while ago, yet every nerve ending in her body was attuned to Mr. Fulton to see what his answer would be.

"Well, it depends on what you mean by know, Miss Smith. She's like a

18

kid sister. She's very young. I wish Madam didn't have her, to be honest."

"She does seem young."

She noticed Mr. Fulton's jaw tighten. "I pay for her time to talk to her. Sometimes I take her out to eat, even though Milly makes great meals at the house. But, I don't want her 'working' like the others. Unfortunately, there are those who like them young, and I can't buy all of her time."

"That's terrible."

"It is terrible, but that's the nature of some in this world." He put down his punch mug. "One of them is your intended groom, JD. He likes to know her that way, but he refuses to marry you. I find that most interesting."

Avis knew a dark cloud had been lifted from her. "She doesn't look very friendly."

"She doesn't talk. She's mute. So, she's a very good listener."

Avis saw the brown eyes focusing on her and Mr. Fulton and instead of giving in to the dark cloud, she gave a small wave to the girl who looked away.

Her attention was on Madam. She had the same last name as the family she left Avis with back East. Similar hands. Same nose. They both had dark hair. She would have to keep her eyes on her before she confronted her. She didn't want to mess up anything. For now, Mr. Fulton had offered her an opportunity, and she was grateful.

"I think it'll be okay if you show me the store."

"It's Christmas Eve."

"Which means?"

"It's a holiday, Miss Smith. Time to celebrate the birth of our Lord and Savior."

She swallowed the last bite of cookie. "Christmas never meant much to me. I've lived my life as an add-on. An extra. So, I don't see the reason behind it all."

Liam Fulton took a visible step back from her, but Avis wasn't surprised. More rejection. She gave him a smile.

"Well, I'll show you, but I won't expect much work from you. Not today."

"We'll see."

The focused burn of Angelique's eyes was on her back as they left the Christmas gathering to head down the street to the general store.

"Why is it called Cobb's Penn?"

19

"Cobb is my middle name. And Penn. Well, you will see."

Liam stepped in front of the space and swung the door open. Goods and boxes were stacked everywhere. It was hard to make out where the counter was, but at least he had a register to tabulate.

"Penn? Like an animal pen?" Avis tilted her head to the side.

Liam nodded. "When my father died I invested my inheritance into this store to have something to do. I don't really have much of a head for business. I've been studying law on my own. When Noelle becomes a town, I hope to be the town lawyer."

"And you have been making money?"

"Well, yes. I do well. I'm the only game in town."

That could be, but there was no doubt that Cobb's Penn was leaking money because of the shoddy way it was kept.

"You live here?"

"Well, it's my building. See? He stepped over some boxes toward a curtain and pushed it to the side a bit. "I live in the back. It's nothing fancy. I get my meals at Nacho's, but I sure hope his bride is a better cook than he is. I'm getting kinda thin eating his cooking."

Avis stood there, mitts folded, saying nothing.

"What do you think, Miss Smith?"

"Well, I believe that you have saved me. Now, I will do the same in return."

She watched him gulp. His Adam's apple slid over the long expanse of his neck as he stood there staring at her. "What do you mean?"

"If there is a piece of material or scarf somewhere in here, I can show you. I don't want this dust to get on my hair."

He scurried among the boxes and produced a square of calico, handing it to her with a flourish. "Thank you."

Avis rolled up her sleeves, took her bonnet off and tied the calico about her head.

"Before you start, Miss Smith, we haven't discussed your salary."

"I thought you told them you were canceling JD's debt. So, I'll work for whatever the train ticket costs. I don't want to put you out."

"That's for him. What about for you? Don't you need some funds?"

She did. But what she needed now were better clothes. She knew she could get something better from talented bride Birdie Bell, who had helped them get warm clothing, but she wanted to make sure to pay her well enough for any dress goods that she used. "I do. I'll need some money for a new start in Denver. Tell you what."

"I'm listening, Miss Smith."

"I'll work for you through the holidays. It seems as if everything is happening in Noelle right now."

"Well, that's the hope, and I accept. Anyway, we'll see if you are even here that long. I'm certain you will find a husband soon."

Avis sighed. She doubted it. Not now with her secret out. "You said you worked on the Underground Railroad Network with your family. Whereabout?"

"Pennsylvania."

"I see. I was born in New Hampshire. Funny how we ended up here, isn't it?"

"Life can certainly be strange."

"It never made you wonder how folks treated people like me back there?"

"What do you mean, people like you?"

"Mr. Fulton, you know what JD Jones did."

"JD Jones is a fool if I ever saw one. He's mean and spiteful and well, I might as well tell you, I prayed for whomever his bride would be. Musta prayed hard."

Avis nudged aside a box. "Prayed for a stranger? Why?"

"I know he's not someone who deserves a wife. When it happened that he got a straw and I didn't, I wondered if there weren't some purpose to that."

"Well, I know that Mrs. Walters is working hard on getting more women to come out here from Denver. I hope you find what you are looking for in the next group that comes out."

She squared her shoulders. "If you'll excuse me, I'll get right to work."

He brought a timepiece out of his pocket. "I know there will be a service tomorrow night, if you care to join me there."

Avis pushed aside some boxes, making a pathway to get to the register more easily. "I'm not sure if the people of Noelle would want me at such a service."

"It's Christmas, Miss Smith. All would be welcome."

"Some of us from Ham's lineage wouldn't be welcome. Ask JD Jones."

"Well, that's not fair. I'll escort you myself."

Avis stopped shoving boxes. "You would?"

"I would. People need to see that you are going to be a part of things."

"I don't have anything to wear."

"Your dress is fine. Come as you are."

Avis knew she wasn't in good with the Lord. She wasn't sure how well He thought of her showing up on His son's birthday. "Let me get a good start here. I suppose you need me to fix where you live behind the curtain too? Talk about an animal pen."

Liam Fulton took off his broadcloth coat and rolled up his own sleeves. "I can't have you do all of the work, Miss Smith. It's my store too."

"You're paying me, but suit yourself."

Avis turned her mind over to the task of transforming Cobb's Penn. If everyone showed up to the store eventually, then her mother would come in one day, and she would be ready to confront her on her own territory.

CHAPTER FOUR
The First Day—December 25, 1876

It had to have been the most unusual Christmas Liam had ever had. Still, in the way she moved all of the boxes around, that evening and most of the next, her efficiency in opening them and arranging the contents was a revelation.

"Have you ever worked in a store before?" Liam marveled.

"No, I've just looked in a lot of windows."

He didn't hesitate in using the hammer to open the shipping crates things came in.

Avis stood when the shadows dimmed the room. It was five o'clock. "It's not nearly ready, but it's a start."

Liam stood and looked around Cobb's Penn. It looked better than it had when Avis first stepped inside.

"We can finish arranging after the service."

"Or you can go and leave me here to continue to work."

"No, you need a break. We both do."

"We need some dinner too."

"I don't think Nacho's is open."

She wiped her hands on the front of her dress. "Can you spare a tin of soup?"

Liam nodded, "That sounds fine."

"I'll go back here and set it up."

Avis stepped around several boxes and disappeared through the curtain he used to section off his living quarters from the store.

It was as if she had always been there. His place was already better with her presence. If Avis was any indication, these women were really going to change the town into the very thing that the Penworthys were looking for when they wanted marriages: something settled.

"Mr. Fulton," Avis called.

He stepped around the boxes and through the curtain to get to her voice. "This is a mess back here! Why do you live this way?"

"Well, Miss Smith. I got busy with the store, and I haven't had time to make it look more homey."

"You needed a wife more than JD Jones did." Maybe he did.

"Good thing I was able to hire you then."

Her pretty features looked startled for a minute, then she reached out a hand for the tins of beef soup he held. "I'll heat this up. Then we can get going. Will the service be in the saloon?"

"Yes, it's the biggest space. The tree is there now."

He sat on the corner of his bed and watched her bustle around in his living space, heating up the beef soup. This had to be unreal. He would have never thought about a woman being in his space at the beginning of the week, especially not a woman like Avis Smith. She was young, brave, and extremely beautiful. What could have possibly driven her to come this far west? Would she speak to him?

"I see you have some crusts of bread here to go with the soup. But you've got to do better than this. Do you not see the opportunities you have to get more business in here?"

Liam shook his head. "I told you I'm not very good."

"Well, I don't think you are trying very hard, Mr. Fulton."

She balanced two tin mugs full of the beef soup, cut the moldy end off the loaf of light bread and pushed a slice to him.

"I think we should pray for blessings."

"Blessings, Mr. Fulton?"

"You made it here safely."

"I was humiliated in front of the entire town yesterday."

"By a foolish man. No one will care about that. Or him, Miss Smith. Trust me in this. I'll pray."

He was sorry that her journey in life had battered her about so that she had little faith in prayer. Still, he lowered his head once he saw her scarf-covered head lower as well. "Thank you for getting these women through the rough paths safely, Lord. Help Noelle to be a good town, a kind town, so that all who come here who differ will be made to feel welcome here. We ask this in the name of your son whose birth we celebrate today. Amen."

They lifted their heads and looked at each other. She sipped from her mug of soup. The bread was a little hard, so she dipped the edge of it into the soup and then ate it.

"How did you know to do that?"

"It makes it taste better. Try it."

He did, and she was right. "I would have thrown it away."

"Oh no. There's still a lot of life left in that loaf of bread yet." Her voice piped up and then faded away, as if she were ashamed of what she revealed about herself.

"What has brought you all the way to the west, Miss Smith?" Liam sipped from his own mug.

"I have a score to settle, you might say."

"I see. Is it with JD Jones?"

Avis shook her head. "No," she said as she looked around his small living space.

It really was too small to have a wife back here with him. He was lucky he didn't draw this first time. When they drew again for the spring, he would fix the situation. Maybe he would build a house on that piece of land by the lake that he liked.

"Coming to work for you was the best thing to happen. I know how to work hard."

"Hard work is never a problem."

"No, but letting go is." She sipped, and her lips came out to meet the edges of the tin. He hoped her pretty pink lips didn't burn. Where had that thought come from?

"Well, I hope you find what you are looking for. And that you're able to live your life free and independent once you do."

Liam pulled out his father's watch and opened it. "They'll be gathering soon for the service." He drank down more of the soup. "If you need to freshen up."

"We both probably do. I've heated some water here."

She had noticed his basin and anticipated his need. Wasn't that handy? "Yes. Well, you go first then I will."

"Thank you." He stepped to the store side of the curtain with his mug and continued to listen as Avis bustled around behind it. The air was scented with a faint scent of something sweet and floral. What magic had Avis brought into his small world already?

When she stepped to the store side of the curtain, she had freshened her chignon at the base of her long neck. He wished he could have seen her hair, but it would not have been appropriate. She had unpinned the towel from her front. "I'm ready."

"Okay, I'll just be a minute." He swallowed the rest of the soup, which had cooled by then and washed up. He put back on his black broadcloth

Prince Albert jacket and joined her in front of the curtain. "I hope I didn't keep you waiting."

"Not at all."

He offered his arm. "Let's go then."

Avis stepped back. "I don't know if you want to do that."

"Why not?"

"Folks might wonder."

"No, they won't." Liam offered the crook of his arm. "It'll be fine. Trust me, Miss Smith."

She donned her cloak and put her small hand into the fold of his arm. Liam's arm resonated with the warmth of her touch. Just the touch of her small hand was a precious gift. He opened the door to his business, and they stepped out onto the street, picking their way through the snow banks and the clear, cold crisp evening. The saloon was lit up with people and light.

Seamus, the barkeep, had arranged chairs in the same way they did whenever church services were held. However, with the additional population, many men were standing to allow the new people a seat. When Liam and Avis entered, no seats remained. Liam thought someone should get up and offer their seat to Avis, but several of the miners remained firmly in place. Did these louts have no manners? He glared at the lot of them, but Seamus waved to him and pulled forward an overstuffed chair. "There, Miss Smith."

"I don't need to sit in such a fancy place."

Liam patted her hand. He didn't mean to. He just wanted her to be comfortable. Still, the warmth in her small hand went up his arm and into his heart. "Nonsense, the best chair in the place was meant just for you. Please."

She went to sit, and Liam noticed the snippy bride with the blond ringlets sitting nearby. She made some kind of giggle and glared at Avis, so Liam glared at her. She stuck her arm through the crook of Horatio's arm. If that was his bride, Maybelle, mayhem, may something, he deserved what he got.

Chase Hammond went to the front of the room and held his hands up. "Thank you. Thank you for gathering here on the night our Savior was born. It's an important night. Our town is being born with the new arrivals here, and we welcome all of you." His eyes lit on Avis in her special chair in the back. "We're better for you being here. I'm not going to keep everyone here long. I want to read the story of the birth of our dear Savior. Then we can sing. I love

26

to hear the songs of Christmas, and now, we have some pretty voices to add. So, we'll sound better, no doubt."

Chase read the Christmas story in his firm strong voice. The wonder of the events of that night never failed to move Liam. From the lowest of the low came a King to save everyone. The lesson of the story, to be kind to all because you never knew who might be special or have a special nature about them, was always crystal clear. That was why whenever his family worked to help the enslaved people get across the Canadian border, he remembered this story and this Christmas night.

Avis's chin lifted, and she stared at Chase while he read, but her eyes were hard. What had she seen in her young life to make her be that way toward the Word? Maybe if she worked in the store, she would confide in him and he would help her, as he had helped others. It was the least he could do.

Chase closed the Bible. "What song would anyone like to sing?"

They sang choruses of *God Rest Ye Merry, Gentlemen, Good King Wenceslas, O Little Town of Bethlehem, and Hark the Herald Angels Sing.* Liam joined in the music, but noticed that Avis kept her voice low and quiet. Maybe she didn't enjoy music.

"I always enjoy *Silent Night*. Brings a tear to me eye," Seamus said.

"We'll sing that next and then a Christmas surprise," Chase said.

People murmured amongst themselves. What other surprises could this day hold? They started to sing *Silent Night*. Someone had adorned the Christmas tree with candles and lit them. The softened light lent a reverent glow to the saloon where many friends in town had fought, drank, and spat. But tonight, the feeling of human community mattered most. Soon, someone started singing the descant part of the song. He hadn't heard that part since his childhood, but it seemed that somehow, a Christmas angel had landed in their midst. The descant part was high, and it required sustained breath to sing it properly, but this woman, one of the brides was singing it. Liam noticed that everyone else's voice fell away at the wonder of it, much as the shepherds must have wondered at the singing angels on that night almost two thousand years ago. Several of the miners had tears in the corners of their eyes at the sweet sound of a woman's voice rising above them and taking control of it all.

He looked down at the overstuffed chair and understood that it was Avis singing. Avis had somehow transformed the alternate arrangement of the carol to suit her voice. She changed it and made grown men cry at the

27

purity of her voice. He was very nearly one of them.

Long Ago…
The Christmas Eve dances at the Bonheurs were a great deal of work. Avis was little, but she could carry and fold things. Many people arrived in their carriages wearing pretty, frilly clothes, and Avis would stand there watching all of the people, while clutching the hand of her mother who would bitterly opine about why SHE couldn't have a nice dress like that. Avis never understood why her mother was so angry watching the people. It was a pretty show. So many colors and pretty perfumes lit the air, but none of it covered the scent of pine that was the basis of their Christmas. That was the best smell of all to Avis, and because it was Christmas, they would be able to have a special cake or treat. The Bonheurs were kind people and always helped her mother, especially at times when they didn't have enough to eat. At the end of the party, just as the clock struck over into Christmas Day, everyone gathered, including the servants, to sing *Silent Night*. Back then, they sang it in German. Still, there was a lady guest, one special lady whose pretty voice floated high above the melody of everyone else in the candlelit room, and Avis always wanted to be that pretty lady whose name she never knew.

When she heard the poor miners scraping along, singing *Silent Night* in English, she reached for that melody to make it pretty, just as it was in that long-ago time in New Hampshire. The last Christmas she had ever had with her mother.

So, it was very strange that when the song came to an end, everyone in the room stared at her. Warm red blood rushed to her face. "I'm sorry."

Liam reached down and put a hand on her shoulder. The warmth of his hand circulated through her, radiating joy in her like a Christmas miracle. Did she dare hope to be accepted? "That was beautiful, Miss Smith. Very beautiful."

.

She turned to move the chair to the side and saw Liam Fulton regarding her as if she were the Christmas Star dropped down from the sky. "Excuse me, I'm going to put this chair back."

"I can do that," he shook his head from his stupor, picked up the chair as if it were nothing and walked out of the room.

Avis made her way to the brides and stood at the edge of the circle. Never sure if she were welcome. Never sure if she would be rejected. The brides who surrounded Felicity had parted a bit and quieted in front of her. The moment bridging acceptance and rejection was always hard. Which way would it go? Why did it always have to be one or the other?

"Avis." Felicity held her hands out toward her. "Your singing was just beautiful. Have you sung like that before?"

"I don't do it often. I don't like being out in public that way."

The brides murmured their disagreement. They reached out to reassure her they felt differently. Well, except for Maybelle. As expected.

"Your voice is very special." Felicity squeezed Avis's hands.

Avis squeezed back, relishing the feeling of acceptance. "Thank you."

She stepped away from the group and went to Liam who was standing at the bar, quaffing a warm drink. Avis knew it was warm because he kept the mug dancing between his fingers. "You want to stay?"

"I'm for leaving. I've had a long day."

Liam put the tin mug down. "I completely understand. Let me escort you back to your living quarters."

They said goodnight and departed. The Colorado night sparkled, and Avis breathed in the cold night air, marveling at the day.

Mr. Fulton broke the silence. "I have no doubt you'll find a suitable husband. Wait until we reopen. They'll be lined up in droves to marry you, just to hear that pretty voice you have singing lullabies to their babes."

Why did his words stir something unfamiliar deep in her belly? Was that her corset poking her? Why was this man talking to her about babies? What should she say to him? Thank you?

She clenched the mitts on her hands that she really no longer needed, now that everyone in the small town knew who she was. Had she come to be the spoiler in the Noelle settlement? Just to confront the mother who had abandoned her? No. As Mr. Fulton said, she would work in the dry goods store and someone would marry her. Fortunately, it would not be JD Jones.

It could be someone worse, given your luck. The small voice whispered to her. It took everything in her to focus on the potential happiness in store for her and not shudder.

29

CHAPTER FIVE
The Second Day—December 26, 1876

The next day dawned bright and clear. Avis had a purpose that the rest of the brides did not have. She did not have to wait around for her groom to come and court her. She had a job. So, for the first time in her life, she was able to wake at the relatively late hour of seven and attend to her toilet. There was a hot breakfast ready for her to eat when she came downstairs, and she found herself welcomed into a group of smiling friendly faces, including that of Mrs. Walters, who was not at all angry at her, but instead seemed resolved that Mr. Fulton's scheme to get her in front of the community would pay off.

"I absolutely agree with him." Mrs. Walter's kind green eyes sparkled as she patted Avis's hand. "Look at our start already! There's plenty of time to find a husband for you, as beautiful as you are, Avis. Don't worry."

Still, Avis had been in too many circumstances where she had seen worry. She recognized it and knew it as a true friend. She was able to leave the brides filled with hot coffee, flapjacks and crispy bacon prepared by Milly the cook who smiled at her when she offered her a plate. "Liam is a good man, but he can be a dreamer." Milly told her. "If you can help keep his mind on the business, you'll be of great help to him. Lord knows he needs it."

"Oh, I hope so."

Birdie had given her a heavier cloak to wear since she had to go outside. She stepped foot out of the door of La Maison, and when she did, she faced the abandoned saloon where, according to some of the other brides, Madame Bonheur moved in with her girls. What room was Madame Bonheur in? How would she find a way to confront her mother? What would she say?

She had come so far. If only she had the courage to go up to the door and knock. Who would answer? What would they say to her?

"Why do you stare across the street, Avis? Looking for future employment?"

Avis shivered in her cloak and stepped away from the beady eyes of JD Jones, the man who had rejected her. Still, she stood firm. She knew who she was and what she had come for. "My name is Miss Smith."

"You are no Miss Smith, my dear. You're Avis. And when January 6th comes and goes and there's no husband to claim you, well then, you may as

30

well get some employment across the street." His voice was reed thin, not rumbling and comforting like Mr. Fulton.

"How dare you speak to me in that way? Why is it any of your concern? You rejected me in front of the entire town. You've been paid your money in return. You and I don't have to have anything to do with one another." Avis stepped away from him into the street and made her way to Cobb's Penn.

"There's no need of you to be so high and mighty now, Avis. I'll see you come crawling back to me yet. You'll come to me, looking to save your social standing in this town. Only when you come to me, I won't have you to wife. You'll do as I want you to do, without marriage."

Avis stopped in her tracks, her insides threatening to toss up the yummy flapjacks and bacon. "That won't happen, Mr. Jones. Never."

He came close and breathed on her, his hot breath nearly freezing in the air, but not freeing Avis from the smell of his unclean teeth and body, poorly masked by some other sharp putrid scent and the stench of alcohol. "Oh, it will. You just watch. It all turned out better than I had hoped. You're far more beautiful than I imagined, and since you aren't white, I can claim you as I want, when I want. I won't have to shell out any money to Madam. You'll come to me."

"Good day to you, Mr. Jones. I wish that you continue to have sound sleep."

If it weren't so cold, small tears would have started in the corner of her eyes. How could he treat her so terribly? What had she done to deserve this kind of treatment from this horrible man?

"You think you are better than me, don't you? Well, look and know, my Avis. We're exactly the same. That's why you will come to me when you have nowhere else to go."

Rather than avert her gaze from the man, she looked him square in his hideous face and dared to face his beady gaze. Of course. He too had colored blood in his veins. That's how he knew her secret. He was of the same skin tone and shade and had been playing the passing game himself. His thin hair made it so much easier to mask his Negro blood. She opened her mouth to direct him from her path when a shadow fell across them both.

"If you don't stop harassing my employee, Jones, I'll have Sherriff Draven lock you up." Liam Fulton spoke quietly, but there was no doubt he meant every word he said. He reached his hand down and pulled the smaller

31

man from Avis's side, casually tossing him into the slush-filled street.

"You'll have to be your own lawyer when I sue you for injury, Fulton. I'm sure I broke my arm. I'll go to Doc Deane right now and have him look at me." JD Jones ran off in that direction, but Mr. Fulton didn't give him a look at all.

Mr. Fulton stared down at her, and Avis hooded her face as a stiff wind blew from the east side of town. "How are you, Miss Smith?"

"Well enough now, thank you."

She tucked her hand into the crook of his arm in that comforting familiar way. He patted the back of her hand and ensured her bare fingertips were fixed into the crook of his arm.

"Good. I'll walk you to work from now on so you don't have to worry about the riff raff of Noelle speaking to you." They stepped away from JD Jones scrabbling through snow banks to get to Doc Deane. He appeared to be just fine. "Noelle is a fine place, and we want to keep it that way," Liam spoke into the wind, loud and clear.

When they reached the door of Cobb's Penn, Avis couldn't stop a glance back at JD Jones who still huffed and puffed down the street. Then she faced the store, which was still in disarray. Knowing that she had much work to do, she pushed the ugly little man from her thoughts and focused on her present concerns.

There was much less to do than Avis thought. Liam joined in to help her, and by the time it was coming on midday, they were finished. Her sleeves rolled up and apron on, she stood next to Liam, looking about at the fruits of their labor. "Avis, I have to say. This place looks amazing."

She twisted to look upward at him and used a shoulder to give him a bit of a hit. She almost boomeranged backwards at the hardness of his arm. "Oh, go on. Well, actually, you are right."

He laughed as she rubbed her shoulder. Ouch. He was a lot tougher than he looked. Liam was tall and gangly, almost like what Washington's Ichabod Crane must have looked like, but there was real male muscle beneath the stark white shirt he wore underneath his suit to present a clean, neat facade to his buying public.

"Are you hurt?" His red eyebrows gathered as he reached toward the impacted shoulder. "You need to take more care. I expect the journey here was quite tiring. Then compared with what you've been through in your

32

life..."

Avis hadn't heard what he said. No one had ever touched her in a kind way like that. Liam's long fingers lightly massaged her shoulder and sent an unexpected jolt through her. Her knees would not obey her internal command to stand up, for some reason.

Liam's hand moved to capture her elbow, and she righted herself on the counter.

"That's it. I've worked you too hard. We should go get dinner at Nacho's."

Avis's eyes fluttered. She hadn't heard great things about Nacho's, even as Fina had vowed to go into her fiancé's establishment and make everything better. Still, it might be better than the soup they had yesterday.

"I'm okay, but a meal does sound good. I'll tell you what, I'll rest up here. Can you bring something back?"

Her offer broke the hold between them. Liam donned a warm coat. "I'm on my way. When I return, we'll open, and I'll show you how it all works. Will that do?"

The look on Liam's face was so earnest she nearly laughed, but then she remembered his kind touch on her shoulder and nodded.

He made his way out the door, and Avis watched him through the window practically running to Nacho's.

She blew air out of her mouth and perched herself on a barrel of saltfish. She wasn't weak or anything, but Liam's kindness had her feeling a bit wobbly. Why was he so kind to her? Especially after everyone knew of her revelation. Everyone was kind at breakfast, even Angelique who insisted on splitting her time between the two houses and came by to help Milly serve breakfast. Yes, she recognized the caramel-colored skin of the girl and the slight frizz to her hair. A sister. She wasn't as pale as Avis and would never have a chance of passing as she and JD had done. Still, the girl's intense gaze on her was shocking.

Then, almost as if she conjured the girl, her face appeared in the window of Cobb's Penn. She had a perpetual sad look on her face. Had she come to talk?

Avis stood and opened the door to her. "Come in. Come in. Please. We aren't quite open yet, but we will be soon."

Angelique wore a mish mash of brightly colored, loose clothing. She had no coat on. Avis pointed her to the fireplace at the far end of the store near Liam's curtained area. "Would you like to warm yourself?"

The young girl's lips were almost blue. She came inside, and Avis closed the door behind her. The girl strolled to the fire looking all about her as she went.

"Do you like it? We've been working hard to make it look more like a store."

The girl seemed consumed with rubbing her hands in front of the fire.

"I can put some coffee on, if you like."

She nodded. She must not be able to speak. Avis had lived with a mute girl for a short time in New Hampshire, so she knew how to talk to her. She knew if she faced the girl and made gestures, she didn't have to raise her voice to be understood. Avis went behind the curtain and began to make coffee.

She might steal something. Are you crazy?

Avis moved as quickly as she could to put the coffee into the damper and add some of the boiled water Liam kept on the back of the stove to make coffee. But there wasn't enough water, and he had no pump inside. Avis took up the pot in her hand and went back into the store. And, there she was.

Her mother.

CHAPTER SIX

Avis's mouth was open to say she would get some snow or icicles to melt for coffee, but every word was snatched out of her mouth by the appearance of Betsey Smith in the store.

"Well, you must be zee little bride Liam iz taking up. I wonder at it all. He got no straw in zee drawing, but you are here. What would that make you? The leftovers?"

Avis could not speak. The energy of the woman, not to mention the strong perfume of the madam, took over the entire storefront.

"I have come wive my Angeliquey here to see why our Liam haz not been to my La Maison, eh? He has nearly abandoned her. Or did he not tell you he likes to come and zee her?"

Avis knew. No matter what Madam said, she knew Liam Fulton was not coming to see Angelique for the reasons she was implying. Avis knew intimately how there were many men in the world who would do such a thing. Liam Fulton was not one of them. She gave a hard swallow and turned to see a stormy look on Angelique's face. Why was the mute girl angry? Was she angry with her? Or her madam?

Avis's head almost exploded from so many new thoughts. She bent over to pick up the coffeepot. The movement helped to force words from her diaphragm. "What Mr. Fulton does in his free time is his own business, ma'am. Not mine. I'm his employee."

"Hiz employee? You?"

"Yes." Avis put the coffeepot on a nearby counter.

"Why he hire you zeen?"

"I was to marry JD Jones. He rejected me, so Mr. Fulton offered to let me work in the store to pay back the money Mr. Jones paid for my train fare."

The madam laughed, and her laugh triggered an echo of something in Avis's mind. A time when her parents would laugh and dance together in their small cabin in the forest where they lived. Betsey Smith still laughed the same way. But her face, puffed out by comparison and the passing of the years, had clearly known sorrow and harshness. The stark shadows on the face of this woman touched her heart, and Avis questioned if she were doing the right thing by coming here to confront her.

35

"Oh, my dear. Zat is too rich!" Then she stopped laughing and came closer to Avis. "A lovely woman like yourself should not be working in zee store. Still, I admit, it looks better for it. But you need to come work for me! Make money in your zleep, eh Angelique?"

She pulled the girl closer to her, away from the fire. "That's enough." The madam told the girl in quite a different way.

There was one thing Avis couldn't figure out. "Why are you talking like that?"

Her mother only knew one or two French words from the Bonheurs. Why did she have an accent? Her mother's way of speaking was flat. Maybe she wasn't the right woman?

But they had the same large, shiny forehead. Now, Madam's was wrinkled up. "Such a pretty one as yourself should come to zee other house and we speak about it, eh? You could be out of here faster if you come work for me."

A cold gust of air entered the storefront, blowing the heavy scent of Madam's perfume out the door. "Madame Bonheur, what a pleasant surprise."

Avis could tell by the way Mr. Fulton spoke, it was anything but. The tone of his voice gave her some relief, but she could see the way Angelique lit up when he came into the room. It was almost as if the girl had feelings for him. Not the kind of feelings that made sense, if he were having his way with her, but real feelings. What was going on here?

"I see you have someone in your employ, Liam. She's lovely."

"She's temporary. She won't be staying. Like Angelique."

Madam fixed a tight arm around the girl. Poor Angelique looked as if she were caught in a bear trap. "Oh my, no. If you want this one, you'll have to pay for her more than zee twice a week you come, yes? Much more. I have other customers, like Mr. Jones, who are willing to pay so much more when they hit the big strike."

Betsey Smith laughed again, and memories of warmth and arms picking her up in a big bear hug and swirling her around in a dizzy circle came to Avis. She shook her head as she realized Mr. Fulton had put a casual arm around her shoulder. She was warm again.

"We are all waiting for that day, Madame. Every one of us."

"I just bet you are. Meanwhile, Liam, you might want to keep a hold of your lovely prize there." The woman tightened her hold on Angelique. "Just as I've got mine. I mean it when I say she iz quite lovely. If she ever tires of working for you, I have ze offer for her to come to me, yes? Such beautiful skin."

She walked by Avis and touched her cheek. Her mother. Touched her on the cheek. Her knees might have buckled. Had Mr. Fulton not been there holding her up, she would have collapsed.

"You don't have to worry about that, Madam. Avis will be well cared for. She's not going to fall into your clutches."

Madam pulled the reluctant Angelique away. "Come on," she said in a tough, gruff voice.

"Farewell, cherie!" Like magic, her French accent came back, and the two left the store.

Avis shook her head and took a step toward the door. She had plenty to say to Betsey Smith. All of her words had been stored up inside of her for more than a decade, but Liam held her back.

"No. Let the air circulate in here for a bit. We have to get ready to open anyway, and the stench of her perfume needs to clear out of here." He let her go and the cold of the room enclosed on her again.

"I'm sorry. I brought you back Nacho's best beans. They're probably cold again and will need to be warmed up."

"Does she come here often?"

"No, it was quite shocking to see her here. She usually sends Angelique. I must have been away for a while."

"Do you, you..."

Mr. Fulton turned to her, his blue gaze frigid. "Angelique is a child. I wouldn't be able to do that to a child. I'm no JD Jones."

A deep shiver penetrated Avis's bones, and her body fairly rattled. Liam put down the plates of beans and went to the door and closed it. "I didn't mean to make you shiver. My apologies. She won't be coming in here anymore. You don't have to work for her. Look at what you've already accomplished here. I would be a fool to let you go." He strode over to her. "Do you want me to warm the beans up?"

"If she doesn't come back here, how would I see her again?"

Mr. Fulton face cracked with confusion. "Why would you want to see her? Madam is not the best person in the world. She's a bit crazy, actually."

"She can speak in that fake way all she wants to. I know who she is. She's Betsey Smith. My mother."

The pressures of working hard that morning without eating and of seeing her mother so changed all rushed to her head in one swoop, and Avis could not stop herself from slumping to the floor.

CHAPTER SEVEN

It was a good thing he had stood so close to her. He knew he had no business standing so close to a stranger, but everything about Avis Smith screamed that she needed protection. Liam knew that look. He had been brought up to go into action whenever he saw someone with that look on their face. It was why he spoke up. It wasn't just because he hated JD Jones, hated the thought of him being with this beautiful woman, squiring her about town on his arm as his wife. He knew how to protect, from the time he was small and had squirreled away human flesh under his bed, hidden into small closets. So as Avis slumped forward, he had her. He caught her in his arms and took her back to his bed and laid her across it.

He picked up her hand and lightly smacked her wrist a few times, but Avis did not stir. He didn't sell vinaigrettes. He should order some now, with all of these women in town. But, Doc Deane might have one. He might know what to do.

"Avis. Miss Smith. I'm going to get the doc. I'll be right back. Stay there."

Liam ran through his storefront and opened his door. He saw a miner on the street and yelled at him to get Doc Deane to come to the store.

Liam didn't even bother to close the door. The doc would need to get in. He pushed the curtain to the side so Doc would know to come back to his living space. Avis still laid there. What if she were cold? He laid one of his mother's quilts on top of her and picked up her limp hand again. "Miss Smith, wake up."

The miner ran back to him. "He's not there. What's going on?"

"She fainted. I don't know."

The miner stepped forward and laid his head near her chest and applied several sharp slaps to Avis's hands. Far sharper than what Liam had done.

"Hey!" Liam pushed the man to the side.

"It'll help her come around. I had a wife. I know." The miner who had helped him was indignant. "Don't you have any smelling salts?"

Liam shook his head. "No, we haven't needed them. With all of these women in town, we might need some now."

Either the sharp taps on her hands or their near bickering caused Avis's

39

eyelids to flutter open. Both men stood in awe and watched her open her eyes.

"What? What happened? Is it time to open?" They both watched as Avis attempted to sit up rather quickly.

"Wait. Hold on there, Miss. There's no need to rush."

"We need to open." Avis insisted.

"We need to make sure you are okay, first." Liam reassured her.

He looked about the store now filled with miners, all looking toward the back of the store where Avis lay on his bed. They had taken off their hats and stood there in silence. Some of them had the nerve to look prayerful.

Something rumbled deep inside of Liam. It was a strange feeling. What was it about this young woman that made him feel this way? He barely knew her. Why should he care? Yet the sight of her on his bed, something told him, should not be witnessed by the whole town of Noelle.

"What are you all doing here?"

"Is Miss Avis alright?" One of the miners stepped forward. "Word got out she was feeling poorly."

"She's going to be fine. Women faint." The miner said. Liam did see that happen twice the other day. Maybe he was right. Still, should he ride out to find Doc Deane?

"She sang so purty," Another one said.

"She look purty too," One of the men said.

Liam drew the curtain and stood in his doorway. "You heard the man. Women faint. She's fine. You all get out of here."

"She fix your store up, Liam? Cobb's Penn is looking mighty fine these days." Grandpa Gus shoved his way to the front.

As always, Grandpa was right. "Yes, she did."

"Now that we can see what you got, I got some things to buy." A miner said and started to give an order.

Liam looked over his shoulder and saw the curtain was still closed. Well. Avis was resting. Nothing to do but get to work. The crowd of miners in his store, buying things and asking after Avis, kept him quite busy for the next hour. Once all of the miners left, some of the brides came through. Word got around quick in this small town. He met a few of the brides who also asked after his goods and put in orders for things they might want. One of them made a quick turn and knocked down a display of cans. Someone called her Bad Luck Penny under their breath, but Liam reassured her it could be put to rights.

Once everyone cleared out, he pulled back the curtain to see Avis sitting up on his bed, scraping the plate clean of Nacho's beans.

"Well, it's good to see you are up."

"I'm sorry to trouble you." Avis rested the plate on her knees. "I was here to help."

"Oh, you helped. This is one of the best days I've ever had. I've been in the back consumed in my law books, assuming people didn't want to buy. They didn't want to buy because they couldn't see what I had. All of that has changed thanks to you. So, thank you, Avis, and take it easy."

Avis stood, and he rushed to her side, but she waved him off.

"I'm fine. It was just the shock of the day. That's all."

He remembered her words before she had slumped in his arms. "The madam is your mother? Really?"

Avis nodded and looked off to the side. "I've been looking for her for a long time. She left me behind when I was six. Today was the first day she touched me in fourteen years."

Liam stared. His mother was an upstanding Christian woman, still working to help the poor in Philadelphia. He couldn't imagine what it would be like to have a woman like Madam as a mother. "She didn't know you?"

Avis gave a little laugh. "I don't think so, but she clearly didn't recognize me. I guess I look very different from when I was six."

"You're only twenty?"

Avis nodded.

"I thought all of the brides had to be twenty-one to make the trip."

She gave a sigh, and Liam tried not to notice the way her apron covered bodice rose and fell with her breathing. It had been a long time since he had a woman. And not one of Madam's women either. "I'll be twenty-one in a few days. Not that Mrs. Walters knows." She covered her face with her hands. "There's so much I've said just to get here to see my mother. Maybe vengeance isn't worth the price required."

"Vengeance?" Liam was captivated now. "Could you explain?"

"We might have customers." Avis looked toward the door and the winter dusk falling outside. Liam laughed.

"You have the right frame of mind for a storekeeper. It was a lucky day that I hired you to be my employee. I've never had the right temperament."

"You're studying to be a lawyer." She gestured towards his law books.

"That's something special. Noelle will need that if it is to grow."

He nodded. "True. For now, I'm a dreamer and an incompetent storekeeper."

"You don't have to worry about it. I'm here now."

A silence fell between them, and Liam noticed the way her lips rounded out the words she had spoken. "I'm grateful, Miss Smith. More than I can say. When will you be twenty-one?"

"On December 31."

Her response caused the precarious nature of his heart to go tipping over the edge. Why was she going back to Denver again? "You say the madam abandoned you? Do you think you have a case against her?"

Her usually graceful countenance changed, and that special glow came back on her face. "A legal case against her?"

"I don't know. You would have to tell me the details."

So, over the next few hours, in between customers, Liam heard Avis Smith's life story. He would have thought she would leave out some details, but no, she told him everything. Some things were horrifying to hear. She had a lot of potential cases against a number of people. He knew the horror of her life when he had seen her beautiful face. Now he understood it. This one woman, this lovely songbird had been prey to all kinds of ugliness in her life. All because the madam had not cared to be her mother. Just because of who her father had been.

Liam usually closed Cobb's Penn when it suited him. Avis's company meant the store stayed open, so he was surprised when he looked at his pocket watch and noticed it was nearly 10:30 at night. "My goodness. I guess we have been talking long enough. Let me show you how to close out for the day."

He pulled out his accounting books and showed her how to make note of barter and money. He noted her swiftness in adding long columns of figures. Her mind was sharp. She figured out the day's deposit ahead of him. Yes, God had certainly blessed him with a gift on Christmas Day when he hired Avis Smith. When everything had been put away, he made ready to walk her back to the house.

"You don't have to do that, Mr. Fulton."

"I most certainly do, Avis. And, I intend to keep doing it, no matter how long you are here. You've had quite a day." He didn't want to add that JD Jones could be lurking close by. It was best this way.

He helped her put on her long winter cloak and noticed how carefully she donned her mitts. "You like to keep your hands warm?"

"Yes," she said, and the look on her face changed to one of thoughtfulness. Liam closed the door to his shop and invited her to put her hand into the crook of his arm.

"Your fingertips should stay warm too, Miss Smith."

"Thank you." She said quietly and did as he suggested. He noticed the careful way she kept her gaze lowered as they walked together. It was cold, as any December day should be, but Liam wasn't noticing it with the gentle press of Avis's hand on his arm. Her touch felt good and right. He hadn't really given much thought to how alone he had been since the cruel death of his fiancée back in Pennsylvania during the war.

They took small careful steps. He didn't want to rush her, given how much had happened to her. Something in him warmed at being in her company, and he was reluctant to rush dropping her off.

"Here we are." Avis announced all too soon as he waited in front of the door of La Maison.

"Yes, I will be here for you at 8:30 in the morning to walk you to work."

Her pretty lips opened just a fraction, in protest, he supposed. He laid his finger on them. The warmth of her moist lips made contact with his finger, and the heat of her breath passed through him like a ripple on a lake. "No protesting, Miss Smith."

"Yes, Mr. Fulton. Thank you." The door opened, and a chattering gaggle of females pulled Avis inside and shut the door. Well, she would be well taken care of without him.

He turned from the door and started the walk back to Cobb's Penn. As he crossed the street, he saw a window shining with light from the abandoned saloon across the way. The lamp was extinguished when he looked up at it. Who was watching him? Was that person more concerned with him or with Avis? It did not matter. He would protect her regardless.

CHAPTER EIGHT
The Third Day of Christmas-- December 27, 1876

Avis awoke in bed, knowing she should have been chilled since the rooms upstairs in La Maison did not have heat. Yet, she felt warmed by the prospects of the day. She had a place to go and a task to perform.

She lives here in this house. Aren't you going to look at her room?

Mrs. Walters had said Madam's room was off limits to them. It was too much for anyone to stay in, the brides had been told.

So, no. Avis was not at all curious about looking in her mother's room. She wanted another glimpse at the actual woman who had offhandedly recommended that she become a prostitute.

Thank the Lord for Liam Fulton coming in to disabuse her of that notion.

She swung her legs over the side of the bed and paused. How had those thoughts come into her mind? To thank the Lord. She was not interested in joining forces with a higher power. It was better to keep things as they were.

And, of Liam Fulton? He was her employer. It seemed though, in his kindness and the way he protected her, that he was also a friend. Something she had never had before.

Avis completed her toilet swiftly, not wanting to keep Mr. Fulton waiting on her for any reason. She donned the black dress again and made her way to the kitchen to grab some early morning breakfast. To her surprise, Mr. Fulton was eating a plate of eggs and bacon and helping himself to a basket of biscuits. Milly appeared to be in her element feeding him.

"Isn't he just wonderful?" Milly marveled. "Look at how he eats all of that and still stays scrawny. The bride you get had better know how to keep up with you, Liam Fulton."

"You know no other woman they brought to this town can hold a candle to you, Milly." Mr. Fulton took a swig of coffee and the woman turned three shades of red.

"You stop that, Liam Fulton. The woman who ends up with you will have a burden to carry on her shoulders for sure." Avis folded her hands and stood in front of them, wanting to burst into laughter at their comfortable teasing. What a nice thing to have a friend.

"Good morning," Avis said to them.

"Hah, Miss Smith. Is it you who has to take on this red-haired devil all day? Let me get you a nice plate. You need your nourishment to deal with him!" Milly scurried away laughing to herself.

Avis came around the other side of the table. "You're here bright and early."

"Well, I just wanted to make sure I was here when you woke up. You're up early yourself."

"I'm an early riser. Apparently, not too many of the brides are." They were the only ones in the dining room. Milly bustled out to them with coffee and a full plate, giving both to Avis.

"Eat up, Miss Smith. You're too thin as it is. When you get married, you'll be making babies and they need to live off of your fat."

"Thank you." Avis told the good woman. With their brows furrowed, she and Liam watched Milly enter the kitchen. Then they looked at each other and burst out laughing at the exact same moment.

"In all my years at college, I had never heard that babies feed on the fat of their mothers." Liam declared when he got a breath.

"I never went to college, and I've never heard that either."

They covered their lips with their hands. "I hope we didn't wake anyone up." Avis whispered.

"Let me bless the food quickly, so we can eat and be on our way."

Avis fixed him with a look. What was the point in that? Still, Liam bowed his head and so did she. The smooth calm in his voice helped to steady her a bit. Then he looked up at her and pointed to the food. "Milly's eggs are the best."

"I disagree. I think her biscuits are the best. They're amazing."

"No wonder Madam's girls have a lot of roundness to them. You'll look like them in no time." Liam's voice slowed as he spoke. Avis quietly spread her napkin in her lap. "I'm...I'm sorry, Miss Smith. I didn't mean..."

Avis reached for the apple butter. "What do you mean, Mr. Fulton?"

"I meant that you just might gain weight. To build you up. I didn't mean that you were going to be like Madam's girls."

"Of course not. I work in your store."

Her employer let out a huff. "Whew. I'm glad I didn't offend you. I just... Well, I think Milly has a point. You are rather thin."

Avis ate heartily of her biscuit and drank her coffee. "I've had precious little to eat in my life's journey. It's something to finally be able to eat high on the hog instead of feeding on scraps like a lower order animal."

"And all I offered you was soup when you first got here. I'm going to have a word with Nacho. I'll see to it that you eat better today."

"After I eat this breakfast, I should be fine until supper."

Liam stood. "Not another word, I'm your employer. Even though I'm not used to having an employee, I'll make sure you have a good midday dinner. I'll be right back."

Avis wanted to stop him, but she was telling the truth about her plate. Minnie and Mrs. Walters came down to join her for breakfast, and they began a wonderful conversation about Culver and Kezia's marriage the day before. "I knew he was a goner when he saw her," Mrs. Walters said as she sipped her coffee.

The atmosphere was warm and wonderful. It was as if her life were finally real and not some horrid stage show people liked to watch. Avis finished her plate and was in the middle of laughing with Minnie about something Maybelle said when Liam reappeared in the dining room.

He gave a little cough, and she stood. "Excuse me, ladies. I need to report to work for the day. I'll see you all this evening."

The three ladies were all quiet as Avis followed Liam into the hallway. Avis reached for the warm cloak Birdie had given her. "Here, let me help you." Liam's hands hovered inches away from her shoulders as if they were a fire. He draped the cloak lightly on her shoulders and turned to open the door.

Avis heard a few giggles from the overhanging balcony. "See you tonight, Fina," She called out as she went through the door.

The door shut behind them.

Mr. Fulton seemed to take no notice of the other women as he watched Avis don her mitts. "There's a beautiful Colorado sun. Wait until you see it in the spring, Miss Smith. It's breathtaking." He held out his arm, and she rested her hand in the crook as she did the day before. "I don't know what is wrong with me. You won't be here in the spring."

"No, I won't." Something in Avis shrunk. There was nothing for her in Denver to return to. Her last employer was just awful. No one had ever been as kind to her as Mr. Fulton.

They progressed to Cobb's Penn in silence and remained that way as they opened up the store for the day.

The traffic of the morning slowed down a bit near midday, and Avis pointed to a cut out panel on a far wall. "Mr. Fulton, what is that?"

Her employer looked up from his desk in the back, his red hair going every which way. She had noticed he grasped and twisted it as he read his law books. What an amazing thing he was doing, sitting back there getting ready for his law exams. She hated to interrupt him with her question, but she wanted to know.

Mr. Fulton looked up at her, almost dazed by her presence. "That's... Those are steps to the upstairs."

"You have an upstairs?"

He shook his head, almost as if he had cobwebs in his mind and kicked up his feet toward the stove. There were holes in his socks, Avis noted, and it took everything in her not to blush and look away. "Why yes. It's slow right now, and it's almost time to eat. If you care to go exploring, feel free. I can take a break and take care of customers."

He walked over to the cut out on the wall and pulled down a set of stairs. "Mercy. How handy."

"Watch your step, Miss Smith." He held his hand out and helped her up. "There might be a little critter or two up there, if you're squeamish."

"I'm familiar with such creatures, Mr. Fulton, but I'll take care."

She didn't know why, but she gave his hand a little squeeze of reassurance as she climbed the stairs, taking care to still her skirts. When she reached the top, there was another floor the entire length of the store filled with all sorts of goods. "Have you taken inventory up here, Mr. Fulton?"

She turned and stared down at him. His handsome face peered up at her. "Not in a coon's age."

"This is all part of your stock. You have to sell this stuff too."

"I know. I know."

Avis balled her hands into fists. Her fingers itched to get ahold of her notepad to tabulate what was up here. She walked around all the boxes stacked up high on the strong sturdy floor. The building was well built. Something occurred to her and she ran back to the opening. Avis could hear Liam conversing with a merry customer downstairs.

"Fina? Is that you?"

Fina's face appeared in the opening. "Aye que, chica. What are you doing up there?"

"Taking inventory," Avis said. "What about you?"

"Delivering the dinner Mr. Fulton ordered from Nacho. I hope you both enjoy it." Fina waggled her eyebrows, and Avis waved a hand at her. "I'm going back to the restaurant now. I'll see you tonight, Swan bird."

Avis looked around at the cartons. She would need to put a real apron on to deal with all of the dust up here. She heard Liam Fulton's step come up the stairs where he stood half in and half out. "There's a lot of dust up here."

"There's a whole world of possibility up here! You could clear all of this out, make money on it and live up here for one."

He came fully up the stairs and stood next to her. "I could?"

"You don't see that?"

"Well, I just lived downstairs because it was quicker to get to things, but now that you're here, Miss Smith, I see what you mean."

"It's nearly worse up here than it was downstairs. I'll need a new apron just to deal with this."

"I can get you one."

"Thank you."

"What else will you need, Miss Smith?"

"My notebook for one. To take an inventory."

"There's one around here somewhere." Liam played with his red hair as he looked around for something.

"Mr. Fulton, you are a lost cause." Avis couldn't remember when she had laughed so much.

"Well, I'm just glad you are here to help. But come. Let's eat while our dinner is still warm. I won't have it be said of me that I overworked you."

She turned from the mess and tried to go downstairs first, but her skirts were too wide. She held them down, but that didn't seem to help. "Oh my."

"Wait. Let me go first, and I'll help you down."

Avis moved aside so he could go down the stairs, but then she saw a different dilemma. If he helped her, he would be able to see under her skirts. She opened her mouth to express her concern, but he spoke up. "I won't look. I'll just stand here with my hand held out. Think of me as a cane, Miss Smith. No more."

Something in her wished that Mr. Fulton might think of her as something more. Then she might be able to stay in Noelle. As she stepped down the stairs, daintily, she could see that was not a possibility. No use in wishing for the family she once had. She had a purpose in coming here. She needed to keep it in mind and not ask for anything else.

CHAPTER NINE

It had been a coon's age since Liam Fulton had the opportunity to look under a woman's skirt. From what he could recall, some of the undergarments were quite frilly. Maybe he should sell such things. Still when he thought of Miss Smith in that way, something pervaded his mind that his thoughts were not at all just or reflective of someone with the right moral character to be a lawyer.

His hand felt moist every time he reached for her small, capable grasp. He refrained from wiping his hands, but would try to air dry them instead. She was splendid in so many ways. How could she not see it?

"What did Miss Fina call you?"

"Some of the brides called me a swan bird because of my singing at the service. I don't know why."

"It's the perfect name for you. Your neck is so... Well, pardon if I say, but elegant."

"Thank you, Mr. Fulton. I don't think of my singing as my last song though."

"Oh. A swansong can mean a song before a transformation too, not just death."

"Well, that's a relief." Avis smiled and reached around him for her notebook. "I have this inventory to take, after all."

He stood there, rooted to the spot, looking at her beauty fill his store. "Why. Yes. I mean. Let me get you that apron."

"And expense a duster as well. There's quite a lot of dust up there, but I'll put it to rights."

"Gladly." Liam fetched her the items she was looking for. "But, first, time to eat."

He escorted her back to the table in his small living quarters, and they ate quickly of the beans and tortillas Nacho had made. "These beans had a little more side meat than usual." Liam tried to break their silence with some conversation. He could never sound right around this amazing young woman. "I hope this food helps you gain some extra padding. I mean weight. It can be a cruel and cold winter here."

"Why did you come here, Mr. Fulton?"

"For the gold strike. Like everyone else. Then when it didn't pan out and my father died, I took my inheritance and used it to buy a store. I recalled well what they said about the California gold strike in '48. The people who made the most money were the ones who had a service or sold things to the miners. Not the miners themselves."

"Well put," Avis nodded. "It's a prime business opportunity."

"I've done very well," Liam nodded.

"It's remarkable how well you've done. And you'll do even better once I get all of the inventory organized." She scraped her plate with her fork and sat back. "Done."

"None of Nacho's pan dulce?"

"Maybe later."

Avis stood and went to the stove. "I'll make some more coffee and then get started. Can't sit around all day."

Liam wiped his plate with the last of his biscuit. "I'm the boss. Doesn't what I say count?"

She threw her head back and laughed. "It's a wonder you made any money, Mr. Fulton. You're too kind to your employee."

Liam pushed his pan dulce close to him, digging a fork into the crumbly pastry. "Well, I've never had an employee before. From the looks of things, you're the best employee ever." He took a bite of the dessert, and the sweetness of the bread spread over his tongue.

"No one has ever been as kind to me as you have, Mr. Fulton. I'm grateful. I want to help make sure Cobb's Penn is the best it can be." Avis gathered up their plates. "I'll clean up, now that you've made short work of your dessert."

"Thank you, Miss Smith."

She put her pan dulce into the icebox keeper and brought Liam a cup of coffee, before preparing a cup for herself. "I still don't see how you live back here. It's not the best circumstance to help you study for your exams. When will that be?"

"In the spring, when the next group of circuit judges come riding this way. It's an oral exam that will take several hours."

Her eyes grew wide, and Liam liked that look in them. It made him feel as if he had done something right for a change. "What will happen to the store then?"

He shrugged. "I'll just close up for a few hours, I suppose."

"I suppose I'll be gone back to Denver then."

They grew silent as they sipped their coffee, captive in thought. "Who is in Denver?"

A few weeks ago, he would never have been so bold, but he had to know. "Excuse me?" Miss Smith said, her cupid's bow lips all scrunched up. *Just perfect for kissing.* He shook his head. Not moral at all.

"Someone live in Denver you going back to? Madam is your mother. You told me that. You were coming out here to marry JD Jones. That's not going to happen. So why are you headed back to Denver?"

Her small hands were curved around the cup. "Well, I guess I hadn't thought ahead like that. I was so intent on coming out here to see her and let her know I was in the world. I really hadn't thought much beyond that."

"So, let me get this straight. You're busy making money to return to a place you don't know why you are going back to? Miss Smith, you seem to have a lot more sense than that."

"Well, everything is so undecided now. I guess my thoughts just ended at meeting her. I hadn't even thought of what it would mean to be married."

"I see." Liam took another sip of the cooling coffee. "So, when are you going to tell her?"

"Since she didn't recognize me? I don't know. I'm a little disappointed to be honest. Something in me… I thought… I believed she would know me."

Her large brown eyes welled up, and Liam could hardly stand seeing her upset. He handed her his handkerchief from his pocket, and she dabbed at her eyes. "As you said, you look quite different than when you were six, Miss Smith."

She gave a little laugh and nodded. "I do. It was just, so much of a dream. I supposed my plan wasn't fair to Mr. Jones."

"Fair to Jones indeed. He's a snake. God has let this all work out the way that it was supposed to. If I could just get Angelique out of his clutches."

Avis put the handkerchief down that had been one of his father's. "You really care for her, don't you?"

"She's a child. Most of us. Well, a number of us around here, buy her time just to have someone to talk to. Hugh over there, the assayer, me, some of the miners. She shouldn't be used that way." A picture formed in his mind, a terrible picture. "The only one I know who confesses to using her in that way is Jones. I've hated him since."

Avis lowered her head. "There has to be some way. Maybe she could come work for you here!"

"You heard Madam. She has charged an exorbitant fee to release her. I'm making money, but it's not like that."

"It's not fair." Her voice took on a hard edge. "The thirteenth amendment outlawed slavery."

"Very good, Miss Smith. But your mother. Well, she has other ideas."

"Maybe I should approach her."

Liam eyed her. "You should approach her for your reasons. Not ones that involve her girls. That's what you came here for."

Avis drank the rest of her coffee. "Something has to be done." She stood and took up the cups. "I'll finish cleaning and then get started. The sooner I can get done the better."

She scuttled all around him, tidying his bachelor living quarters, before going upstairs with her notepad and a hammer.

The afternoon was slow except for when Molly Norris came to the store, but he was pleased with the progress Avis had made. She made several trips downstairs, filling his store with merchandise, setting up mountainous displays of canned goods and such. By the time the sun went down for supper, the store shone. Avis, on the other hand, was dusty from head to toe. On her last trip downstairs, he declared, "You're a mess," and touched the top of her head where some kind of webbing appeared. He was instantly struck by how soft and sleek her black hair felt under his fingertips. "Stand still." Liam hoped there were no spiders in the webbing. "Just cobwebs." He removed the webbing from her head and gathered them in his fingers to place in the trash can.

"Mr. Fulton," she said. "Could you throw those away outside? I don't like spiders."

Liam regarded his employee who stood there, motionless. Her face transformed from its healthy tan color to something several shades paler. "Why, Avis," he asked. "After everything you have done for the store so far, I'm finding it hard to believe you have this fear."

He took the webs outside, shook them from his fingers and stomped on them for good measure. When he returned, Avis looked a lot better. "Thank you." She took off her apron, but there was so much dust on her, the apron left an imprint underneath her black dress. "Oh dear."

She wouldn't be able to wash and dry such a dress or her apron in time for work tomorrow.

53

"I have some leftover dresses that were traded in by some women. I'm thinking they may be a mite big for you though."

"I can fix them. I've always had to alter any clothes anyone gave me to fit."

Liam retrieved the clothes from behind a curtain. The prints were horrible, but he offered them to her. "I should take you home. You've done so much for me today already."

"How much do I owe you?"

"Oh no. This is part of your pay. Please. I just gave you an advance, is all. Please. Take them, and I pray you can figure something out. Now that Birdie Bell is here, I think you ladies will have far better dresses than those."

Liam grabbed his coat and her cloak. "Should I put it on you?"

A mask of worry crossed her pretty face. "No, it might get dirty."

"Take my coat."

"I couldn't, Mr. Fulton. I'll just—"

"I don't care. I have others." He placed his black broadcloth around her shoulders and retrieved his brown hunting jacket to wear. He shut down the store and went out to her. Once again, he offered her his arm. And once again, Avis took it as they strode together down the street with Avis carrying the dresses over one arm.

The silence between them was full and complete. It was as if they were speaking with their souls. Her fingers connected to his arm, bonded somehow. When they reached the front door of La Maison, they could hear a lot of chatter inside from the brides. "I appreciate the walk, Mr. Fulton. Thank you."

"You're right welcome, Miss Smith." Something occurred to him, and he needed to apologize right away. "Please forgive me for calling you by your Christian name before. I didn't mean to take a liberty back there. I was just so surprised at your fear. You've had so much to stand up to in your life already. I would have thought you fearless."

"Everyone has something they fear." Avis whispered. "I'll be presentable for work tomorrow. I promise."

Liam disengaged her hand and folded his hand over hers to keep her fingers warm until she went inside. "I have no doubt of that. Good night, Miss Smith."

"Mr. Fulton," she said, nodding her elegant, but dusty head to him. Avis went inside and closed the heavy oak door of the cathouse, leaving him alone in the cold, but warm from her touch.

CHAPTER TEN
The Fourth Day of Christmas - December 28, 1876

When Avis walked into the dining room of La Maison, everyone was sitting around drinking coffee and eating Milly's gingerbread. The spicy smells mingled with baked chicken made her eyes water, but she knew she had to get a bath first. The brides turned and stared at her. "What happened to you, Avis?" Minnie asked.

Milly came scurrying out. "That red-headed Liam Fulton has been having her work all day, that's what! I fed that scamp breakfast this morning. I'll show him a thing or two. I've got warm water going already, dearie. You come back into my room so you can have a bath in peace."

"I can help. I'm done eating anyway." Minnie volunteered.

"I can fill the tub, if the water is going." Avis piped up, but the two women would not hear of it. They filled the tub in Milly's small, but cozy room and left her to soak and wash her hair.

Avis had no choice now. Her hair would grow wavy instead of the sleek straightness she had carefully cultivated with oil and heat. There had been cobwebs on her head, and she couldn't wait to dunk her head and body underneath the water to be free of them. Just to make sure.

She shivered. Yes, mice and rats had been her friends of the night, but not crawly things. She had enough of those kinds of things crawling over her to last a lifetime. She scoured her body hard and washed her hair. Once everyone saw her natural waves, her real origin would become obvious to everyone. Milly might not even want her in her tub anymore.

Minnie came in with one of her spare nightgowns. "Here you go, Avis. What were those dresses for?"

"My black dress got dusty, so Mr. Fulton gave me some dresses he had gotten in trade to make over. It's part of my pay."

Minnie crinkled her nose. "It's not very good pay."

"They'll have to do for now. It's all I have." Avis held onto the nice cake of lemon verbena soap Milly gave her so it didn't slip away. "I would ask Birdie to make me something but…"

"She's quite busy with Jack Peregrine, I know. Something tells me the two will marry soon. It's wonderful how it's happening, isn't it?"

Avis nodded, and Minnie smiled. "You finish your bath and leave it to us. We need something to do anyway."

Avis was a little mystified, but said nothing. She stepped out of the tub and dried herself off completely before putting on the nightgown. She wanted to dump out the tub, but Milly came in. "Don't worry, dear. I'm looking to take a bit of a scrub myself. It's alright."

Putting on her boots, Avis went out to the parlor where some of the brides were gathered, already cutting up the dresses and pinning pieces on Angelique. "There she is."

Something in Avis's heart started beating. She looked at Angelique's face. The girl was smiling, happy to have the dress pieces pinned on her. "She's about your size, Avis, so we got started without you."

"That's okay. What can I do to help?"

They pressed the prints, reversed the pieces and cut them down to size to make a smaller dress. There was practically enough material to make another dress, but when the clock struck eleven, Avis cried foul. "This will work. Thank you so much everyone. I'll wash my black dress tomorrow."

In all, it had been a good day's work. Angelique waved goodbye and stepped out into the cold, hurriedly making her way across the street to the abandoned saloon. Back to her mother's side.

Avis sighed and blew out the last oil lamp before heading up the stairs to get her own good night's sleep. She had to summon the courage to talk to Madam. Tomorrow.

Mr. Fulton was a little late the next morning. When he did arrive, Milly glared at him as she dished out oatmeal. "Don't you be working her too hard now. Got your nose in all of those books. She came very far to become your wife, Mr. Fulton. You can show her some respect!"

As they left, the woman's harsh voice sounded after them and echoed onto the street. Liam turned to Avis in confusion. "Haven't you explained to her that you were JD Jones's intended?"

"No, I try not to talk about that."

Liam sobered as he took her hand and tucked it into the crook of his arm. "Ahh. That's something I can completely understand."

"You don't like him, do you?"

"My answer doesn't reflect the moral character of a lawyer, but I cannot lie. I do not."

"Me neither." Avis breathed.

"Well, that settles that." They laughed and quickly went across the street to open the shop for the day. They stayed busy all morning long.

When Fina came swinging through the door with their meal pail, both Avis and Liam sat down on barrels looking spent. "Ahh, look at the pair of you sitting there looking hungry. Good thing Nacho has obliged you. What happened to the stock?"

Avis gestured behind her to the empty spotty shelves she had taken great pains to organize. "We've sold it."

"That's what it's there for right? Well, this bean soup and pan dulce will definitely fortify the two of you."

"I would have never been able to sell so much if it hadn't been for Miss Smith. She's been wonderful."

Avis bowed her neck a bit and gave a half smile to Fina, whose black eyes snapped and shone. "Ahh. Yes, she is. I understand now. Well, I have some other orders to fill. I… Adios." Fina fairly danced from the room, and they both looked at each other, eyebrows furrowed.

"I wonder what she is so excited about."

"I'm sure she's rushing back to her Nacho. I think they are falling in love."

Liam nodded his head. "That's wonderful. It'll be even better if she can cook something other than beans."

Avis could see his point. She had only been here four days, and already she was tired of Nacho's beans.

They stood. "Well, I'm not sure what we should do."

"We restock. It's back upstairs with us."

Liam pulled down the stairs. "Back to the dust we go, as they say."

Laughing, Avis climbed the stairs and continued to hand stock down to Liam who set it aside for her to arrange.

They worked hard for a few hours and at one point, Liam went the window. "Now that's odd."

"What?"

"It's Madam. I don't know where she's going."

Avis clambered down the stairs. Her skirts in her new dress were substantially smaller because she only wore her slips and long johns to bustle them out, so she didn't have to worry about appearing unladylike in front of Mr. Fulton. As much as she didn't like the prints, the fit was more comfortable. Liam was there, hand ready to help her down, both watching Madam bustle out of town with something under her arm. "Where could she be going?"

"I don't know, but she's got Birdie Bell's snowshoes under her arm."

"What do you mean?"

"When you were making our meal the other day, I traded those snowshoes for those curtains Abraham snapped up. Why would Madam have them?"

Something inside of her heart beat as they stood there, side by side, watching Avis's mother scurry out of town. What was she up too?

They kept working, but Liam's rhythm had changed as they worked. At one point, hours later, she asked him what was wrong.

"I don't like the looks of any of this. Madame Bonheur is up to something." Liam told her. "I'll be back."

He went for his hunting jacket when she noticed a number of men clustered in the middle of the street. Avis opened the door without a coat on and saw Jack Peregrine was among them. His handsome face scrunched up, and she could tell he was worried about something. "Can you have Fulton come out here please? We need to get up a search party."

Avis bustled back into the store. Liam had donned his coat, rifle in hand. "I heard. Listen, Avis, I want you to close up the store and get over to La Maison with the rest of the brides. Do you understand?"

"I do."

He went outside with the other men. Avis watched the party of men leave and turned to look at the store. Such a disappointment. She was nowhere near finished. What harm could it do if she stayed? Mr. Fulton's words came back to her. She had promised. She should close the store as he said and leave. Still, this was an awful mess to leave behind, and it was bound to discourage more customers. That would be a shame.

"Ahhh, you're still open." She turned around, and JD Jones stood in the front door.

"Actually, I'm just closing up. You might be of more help going with the search party."

The leer he gave her was not reassuring. "What if I see something I want to buy?"

"Put your money on the counter, get it and get out."

"That's no way to speak to a customer, Miss Smith."

"That's no way to speak to a lady."

"Where? I don't see one." He stepped closer. Deep, painful memories from long ago raced through her and made her fingertips ache.

"Please leave."

He picked up a few tins of potted meat. "I'm just buying some things. No harm done."

She blew out a breath and stationed herself behind the register. He put a few more things on the counter in front of her. "That will be a dollar and fourteen cents."

"My, you are a bright one. Aren't you? You have special skills. Makes me wonder what other skills you have."

"Mr. Jones, you made your decision to break our marital contract days ago. You've been properly compensated. I'll take your dollar and fourteen cents now."

"Oh my. You have a lot to say, don't you?"

Avis pursed her lips together and saw the hammer from opening crates on the other side of the counter. *Please God.* If he came for her, she would take up that hammer and do her worst. Nothing, nothing he imagined in his mind was going to happen to her. Never. Not with him.

"You need to take your items and leave, Mr. Jones."

The leer on his face turned stormy. "The nerve of you getting all high and mighty like I'm too good for you. We are one and the same. In fact, I'm the only man you can marry in these parts, missy. You would be fortunate if I ever took you back."

"What do you mean?"

"What I said. Colorado has a law on the books that says whites and coloreds or mulattos can't marry. I've seen that Liam Fulton walking you back and forth like you are special. Don't go getting ideas in your head about marrying him. He's off limits to you. I'm all you've got. And remember, we don't have to get married to enjoy ourselves."

His beady eyes searched all over her body once more as something sank in the pit of her stomach. She suspected as much. Even the law wouldn't let her be accepted. Still, she didn't need to hear that from this horrible little man. With every ounce of strength left in her, she stared back at him and straightened her spine. "Get out, Mr. Jones."

He gathered up the tins putting them in his pockets. "Just put it on my running tab. Liam knows."

She also knew that he had too much credit with Liam, but she didn't care. She wanted him out. As he edged toward the door, Avis picked up the hammer, enjoying the weight of it in her hand. When JD Jones walked out of the store, she locked the door behind him. Liam was gone. There was no one to walk her back across the street. She supposed she would wait until he came back. She turned out the lights in the store, went behind the partition and sat down on Liam Fulton's bed, waiting in the darkness for him to return.

CHAPTER ELEVEN

Thank God Birdie Bell had been found. Everything was going to be alright. Liam smiled as he thought of Jack Peregrine's relief. The man could barely keep his hands from his wife to be, he was so grateful. He shook Liam's hand and invited him to the wedding, but Liam wanted to check on Avis at La Maison.

He was the one who brought word to the women there and was equally grateful they did not run him over when they found out there was about to be a wedding at the Golden Nugget Saloon. He went inside calling Avis's name. No doubt she wanted to go to the wedding as well. Maybe she was helping Milly or something.

"Where's Avis?" he asked Milly.

"Bless me if I know."

"You mean she's not here?"

"I haven't seen her all day. I thought she was at the store."

He swore his heart stopped beating, but he turned on his heel. "I told her to close the store and come here." Milly covered her mouth with her hand.

"If that JD Jones got a hold of her, I swear."

Milly stopped him cold with a hand on his arm. "If he did, you would be the one to blame, Liam Fulton. That woman needs protection."

Liam ran a hand through his hair and picked up his rifle. Law career or not, he would run JD Jones through if he laid a hand on Avis. He went back to the store, praying all the way down the street.

He fetched his door key and opened the door. "Avis! Where are you?"

"I'm back here, Mr. Fulton." The relief he felt couldn't be measured when he heard her voice.

He laid his rifle down and closed the door, locking it. He didn't know if he could manage waiting on customers right now. Not until he had given Avis Smith a piece of his mind for the worry of the past few minutes. He pushed open the curtain and his heart sunk when he saw her sitting on his bed looking downcast, tears obvious on her face. Something inside of him tore apart. "What's the matter? Are you alright?"

Possibilities raced through his mind. She couldn't have talked with

Madam, given her shenanigans of the past few hours. "What's the matter?"
He repeated.

"JD Jones was here."

Liam thought he had reached his emotional bottom until she spoke
those four words. Now, he understood something different. His voice took on
a hard edge. "Did he touch you? He better not have laid a finger on you. Tell
me, Avis. What did he do?"

Horror rose in her eyes. "No. No. He didn't touch me. He proclaimed to
be coming here for some tins of meat, but I think he knew you were gone on
that search party. He said some things to me that... Well... As soon as I earn
enough, I better go back to Denver. There's no point in me staying here."

"What did he say?"

"He said... He said," Avis whipped out the handkerchief he had given
her and wiped at her tear-filled eyes. "He said no one in Noelle would ever
marry me because of who I am."

"Because you are Madam's daughter?"

"No. Because I'm a Negress."

He put his arm around her. "Why are you listening to JD Jones? He's a
fool if there ever was one, Avis."

"Well. He's right. A lot of the miners have been in here and none of
them seem interested in a marriage. Everyone has been very nice, but maybe
he's right. Marriage is another thing. He said there was a law. That I can't
marry anyone because of it."

Liam grasped her shoulders and made her face him. "He said that?"

Avis nodded sadly.

He stood, grasping at his hair. What kind of lawyer was he? Did his
regard for this beautiful woman blind him to all reason in his anticipated
profession? Jones was probably right of course, damn him. Was there a law
in some book he hadn't seen yet? "Look, I wish you would have just gone to
the cathouse as I said. I was worried."

She stood too. "I'm sorry, Mr. Fulton. I didn't mean to worry you. I just
thought you would have figured out I was here. I didn't feel safe going out
after he left since he made a few... suggestions. Because Madam Bonheur is
my mother." He watched her twist and turn the handkerchief in her hand.

He turned toward her. "I want you to know something." Then he
laughed. "Miss Smith, I apologize for the way I keep calling you by your
Christian name."

She giggled a bit. "You've done it quite a lot. You might as well."

"It's a lovely name. Did she give it to you?"

Avis nodded. "It's been my only name."

"It's a bird name. Latin." At least he knew something.

"Ahh. So, when the others call me Swan…"

"It fits." Liam nodded. "Oh yes, Avis. It fits you quite well."

They faced each other, there in the confines of his small bachelor quarters. He had outgrown it already because of this lovely, placid woman who brought order to his life. How could anyone deny her? Why would they? She had never done anything to anyone, except be born in this hateful world. A world he had pledged to make right from the day he was born into it. That had never changed, and it wasn't about to change now. "You should call me Liam."

"No. I. It wouldn't be appropriate."

She had a point. He was her employer. "I wouldn't want to do anything to make you uncomfortable. Not after what you've done for me."

"What have I done, Mr. Fulton?"

He put a finger under her chin. "You've done so much. I could never repay you. I'm extremely grateful. You've more than paid your way back to Denver. You can go back whenever you are ready. If you don't want to stay, then I understand. But you haven't done what you came here to do."

Her eyes blinked. "I know."

It was hard, but he stepped away from her. Her soft face, her wavy locks swept up into temptation on the top of her head, her large pleading eyes… she was too much for him. He missed too much. Colorado was such a new state, with so much potential. It would be wrong for the state to get bogged down into things that simply did not matter.

What if fighting for this woman, this admirable worthy woman, was a way to challenge an unjust system? To show the status quo that everyone deserved a right to happiness? Maybe marriage was the answer.

"Good. When?"

"I'll talk to her in the morning. Before I come."

Her wisdom for one only twenty stunned him. He knew he would be lucky to have her—not the other way around. "Okay. Let's get you back to La Maison. Milly was getting mad at me."

He retrieved her cloak and helped her into it.

"You couldn't help that. Birdie was gone."

64

"She was. Now she's back and marrying Jack Peregrine at this very moment. From the looks of them, they'll be very happy together."

Liam helped her out of the door and locked up his store. They took their normal posture, but this time, Liam kept a hand on hers inside the crook of his arm. He had to make sure her fingertips did not get cold.

When they reached the cathouse, Milly fussed over both of them. "Everyone just got up from supper and ran to the saloon to see the wedding. Folks didn't finish their food. I guess they'll be back. I'll feed you two, I suppose. Although I would be well within my rights to ignore you, Liam Fulton. Leaving this poor young lady behind."

Over supper, they explained the situation to Milly. The good lady sat there, nodding her head, arms folded across her ample stomach. "I see it now. Yes. Well. I'm glad they are getting together. Now, what about you two?"

Avis put her fork down. "Oh my. I'm getting ready to return to Denver. I won't be getting married. My groom doesn't want me."

"No." Milly shook her head vigorously. "He's not for you, dearie. He's an awful weasel, that one. He shouldn't marry anyone. God was looking out for you, that's what."

Liam nodded. "I agree."

"Don't you come in here with all of your agreeing. You could do something about it. You should marry Miss Smith. That would show him up."

"Is marriage something you do to show someone up, Milly? Why don't I just marry you, and then I would be well fed?"

"I see what you are about, Liam Fulton. Don't you think I'm falling for it," She stood. "I'm going to start cleaning up this mess. Too bad for them. There's plenty of pie and cookies if they are hungry when they get back. I can't leave this mess behind. I'm no Madam."

Their plates clean, Avis stood and gathered them. "I'll help her. You go on ahead back to the store. It's been quite a day."

"You've had a series of days, Miss Smith. I mean Avis. And another before you. Do you need company?"

She shook her head. "No thank you. I better go see her myself. I've put it off long enough. I guess part of it was I thought I would be here longer. I worked myself out of that, I suppose."

"Without a doubt, you're a good worker."

"I'm still not finished bringing stock down, but I'll finish tomorrow. I promise."

He stood over her. "I have no doubt of that. Thank you so much for all of your help."

"Thank you for your protection. Good night, Mr. Fulton."

He nodded at her, wanting to make sure to pay her the fullest of regards, given what she had to face in the morning. "Good night, Miss Smith."

Liam left her behind looking forlorn. He wanted to grasp the hair clean out of his head. Some lawyer he would make. But then, he really couldn't beat himself up. He hadn't come to study that part of the law yet, but he would. What kind of territory or place was Colorado to start out with such a prohibition on the books? Was it a territorial prohibition? There were no laws like that in Pennsylvania. But then, his home state won no prizes. Pennsylvania had slavery at the beginning of its founding as well, until it discovered that the institution would not take root and was done away with. The people in his family had been working toward ending the evil for more than one hundred years and had finally succeeded. Now, with his new life here in Colorado, Liam felt as if he were starting that battle all over again. What would it take for this country to wake up and realize the gift they had in those who had come from the African population?

He put on a pot of coffee when he got home and unwrapped the package of spice cookies Milly had pressed upon him. He stood before his stack of books. Something had to be here. Something had to exist to combat the foolishness of such a law. "No colored or mulatto." Maybe it was because Avis was a mulatta? No. That was skating on thin ice. It had to be something more watertight than that.

What if… What if he did like Milly suggested and asked Avis to marry him? She could look after the store as he studied. Then, once he became a lawyer, they could stay in Noelle with the store. Or if they left, lots of other places would be happy to have such a team, a lawyer and a business woman. Ahh, that might have been where Avis got her business acumen from. Yes. Madam was greedy and evil, but no one could argue that she was quite a business woman.

He bit into a spice cookie and swallowed some coffee. Time to get to work to find a solution. If nothing else, beautiful Avis Smith deserved an answer to her predicament before the law.

CHAPTER TWELVE
The Fifth Day of Christmas-- December 29, 1876

This day seemed like all the other days Avis had ever since she came to Noelle. Cold, waking up to the chatter of some of the ladies. However, now that Birdie was married, the house was a bit quieter without her whirlwind energy occupying La Maison. It struck her that the real purpose of them being here in Noelle was to get married, and so many of them had been successful.

This day, though, she was going to confront her mother. This day was the day she had waited fourteen years for. Ever since Betsey Smith let her go in to the Bonheur house all alone. She had told her she wasn't going to work for the Bonheurs anymore, and that she would be back to get her. Told her that she should be a good girl and she would be back. Her stomach got that familiar ache again when she remembered waiting and waiting and waiting for a mother who never came back for her.

Since her black dress was not yet completely dry from the dust, Avis donned the patchwork print dress again and went downstairs for her bowl of oatmeal, half afraid all of the talk would be about how Madam had held Birdie at gunpoint yesterday. To her shock, the male voice sitting at the table joking around with Minnie and Cara and Mrs. Walters was Liam Fulton.

"What are you doing here?"

"Walking you to work." Liam's blue eyes twinkled with merriment.

"Oh."

Avis ate her oatmeal in silence. When the two of them had scraped their bowls clean, Liam stood and reached out for Avis's hand. "Ladies, we must depart. Thank you so much for the good company."

"You're welcome anytime, Mr. Fulton," Mrs. Walters said. "Such a gentleman!"

Avis gave a wan smile, hoping the oatmeal she had choked down wouldn't come back up on her. The ladies left their breakfast to watch Liam help her with her cloak. "Have a wonderful day, Avis!" Mrs. Walters said. She would certainly try.

When the heavy oak door closed behind them, the frost from the air billowed out of her mouth. "What are you doing here?"

"I wanted to give you support on your big day."

"Oh. Well, thank you, but I would have been fine across the street."

"That might be. Still, JD Jones is a weasel as Milly said. He could be anywhere."

She could see that. They took their normal posture and without a care in the world, walked across the street to the abandoned saloon. Liam entered, and it was clear the ladies were in a circumstance not nearly as comfortable as the one the brides were in. For a painful second, Avis felt sorry for them. Well, until one of them who was scantily dressed came up to Liam and began rubbing her chest on Liam's arm. "Looking for some real entertainment, Mr. Fulton?"

"No, Boum Boum. Avis is here to see Madam."

Boum Boum stopped her rubbing. "We don't need the likes of her in here. She trying to get a job? It's bad enough all of these brides are stealing the men away, making them want to go domestic and all."

Another one, a blonde one, stood next to Boum Boum. The look on her face appeared as if she wanted to strike Avis. "Yeah. Get out already."

Angelique, the young mute girl fought through them both, gesturing that they should leave them alone.

"All right, all right. We know Mr. Liam is your steady. We were just hoping he might want to have a party or something."

"In the morning?" the blonde woman said.

"Whenever." Boum Boum said, as they retreated to their corners, ready to wait for a real customer.

"Miss Smith is here to see the madam." Liam spoke to Angelique, looking her in the eye. "Is she available?"

Angelique backed up and shook her head, vigorously. "She's saying today is not a good day." Liam turned back to Angelique.

Avis stared Angelique in the eye. "She did tell me to come by whenever. From the other day. Remember?"

Angelique gave a little smile and spread her hands. She made a welcoming gesture.

Liam turned to her. "She's saying go ahead. Angelique will smooth your way."

Avis grasped her own hands. "This is it."

"This is. Be strong."

She had no choice, did she? She followed Angelique up a set of rickety wooden stairs. The girl turned right and knocked on the door with a special flourish. "Angie? Is that you? Did you bring me some coffee?"

Angelique escorted her into a room that clearly needed Avis's organization skills. Madam sat on a chaise, wearing a fancy, frilly white robe with a scarf tied around her head. "What the… Oh my. Miss Smith? Have you come to zee me?"

The woman's voice rose up a notch as she took on that fake French accent that Birdie joked about at the supper table before she left to marry Jack Peregrine. Birdie might not have made such fun if she knew the woman was capable of pulling a derringer on her. Would she do the same to Avis when she found out who she was? "Miss Smith, Miss Smith. Clear off zome space and sit down. Welcome. Oh, I love your hair and what you did with it. Such waves. Let me see."

The woman came to her and pulled the pins out of Avis's soft swept up hair. She fluffed her hair out around Avis's face.

Avis closed her eyes and let the Madam do as she pleased. This was her mother. Her mother was fixing her hair. Just as she wanted her to do many times. "Yes. Very lovely. You'll do just fine. There, there my dear. Are you crying? No need for zat. You and I are going to make ze ton of money. I have no need of a gold mine wiz you around."

"You don't have to speak French to me, Betsey Smith."

Madam stopped fluffing her hair. "What did you say?" The woman dropped all pretense. The perfume smell of her, the smell Avis would think of as the mother smell, drifted away from her.

"I said you don't have to speak French to me. I know that's not your language."

Madam whirled on her. "How dare you speak to me this way? In my room? Get out. I don't want you to work for me after all. You aren't that beautiful."

Something in her pressed her to stand. "We have the same last name. Smith. Did you know a James Smith? He was my father. I was born in a small village in New Hampshire."

The words, each one of them, gave her more strength as they came out of her. She spoke them stepping towards Betsey Smith as she uttered them, one at a time. It was as if her words were fists, knocking the air out of her mother each time she spoke a new word. "What? Smith is a very common name. Very common. And my name is Bonheur."

"Yes. You took that name from your employers. The ones that you said would take care of me until you came back to get me. Although you never ever did."

The woman seemed out of breath and fell over onto her large bed covered in wildly colored silk quilts. She reached for a smelling salt on the tabletop and broke it open before bringing it to her nose. Interesting. A propensity to faint. Avis came by it honestly. "Who are you? What do you want from me?"

"I don't look familiar to you?"

The Madam's eyes took on a watery appearance. "No, you don't."

"I don't look like my father? James Smith?"

"No."

"I look like you, do you think?"

Madam smoothed down her bodice. "I don't know what you mean."

"I'm Avis Elizabeth Smith. Your daughter." Her fists grabbed at her patchwork skirts. "You mean you don't know who I am?" It had never occurred to her that she could come to this moment and her mother would refuse to recognize her.

"I knew a James Smith. When I lived in New Hampshire. He. He was a wonderful man. He was the love of my life. The day he died, I died. When I buried him, I buried Betsey Smith."

"And not your little girl, right?"

The woman's voice went to a small whisper. "I couldn't look at you anymore. He was gone, and I couldn't… I didn't want to see your face."

"What kind of woman does that? You should have been glad to have a small piece of him." Avis wanted to scream the words, but something inside of her kept her voice low and quiet.

"Avis, I did it for you. I turned you over to them so you could have a better life. I knew those Bonheur people would never pay me enough good money to live. I had to go back to what I knew."

She reached up and grabbed Avis's mitted hand. "I didn't want you to watch me go back to what I knew. I tried. All of those years Jamie married me, made me a wife, I could live right. But when God took him from me, I gave up."

"So, you blame this on God?" That sounded very familiar to her. "What about your little girl? The one you gave away so carelessly?"

"I knew she would be better off with the Bonheurs. They were rich and could take care of her."

Avis took her hand away. "Well, they didn't. They were mean and cruel. The one thing that kept them being nice to me was you. They treated me as a slave in all respects. It was a chamber of horrors. When I was ten, I left them. I ran away and went on a search for you. I wanted you to know that you had done wrong leaving me there with them. When all I wanted..."

Avis covered her trembling lips with a hand. "I just wanted my mother."

"I'm trying to tell you. You didn't have one. Jamie died, she died."

"I don't understand that kind of love. I don't."

"Well, just you wait, young lady." The madam stood and whirled away from her. "He was the only man who ever treated me as if I were a human being in this cruel world. It pained me that the world only saw his dark black skin and never saw who he was. It was wrong. I knew the same thing would happen if I had a baby with him. But something, something went wrong. I wasn't supposed to be able to have a child. And then. It happened."

Madam turned and looked at her as if she were seeing her for the first time. "You are so very fair. If I had known you would grow up looking as white as you do..."

"I might have been worth keeping? Or whoring out? Which one?"

"That is not fair, Avis. That is not fair!" Madam screamed in her shrill voice. The more she screamed, the quieter Avis became.

"I don't care what is fair. It wasn't fair that you left me with those people, and they treated me worse than their dogs. And then when I started developing, growing up, looking like a woman, they passed me around. You knew that would happen. And you left me there."

"It's better to be passed around to some men than to every man. I wanted to give you a chance."

"Well, thank you for that. Thank you."

They had been so consumed in confronting one another, they didn't notice Angelique had come into the room until she put her hands between them to keep them apart. Madam gave a little laugh. "Don't worry, Angie. I'm not gonna hurt her. Not this one."

Angelique nodded and made some gestures. Madam looked at her intently. "Yeah. I guess she is kinda like your sister. In a way."

So, Angelique knew too. The hallmarks of blackness were like a code they could see in one another. Avis nodded and grasped Angelique's hands, stepping away from them both.

"What do you want from me?" Madam's countenance was low and dragged down, as if she had been in a prize fight. "Money?"

"I don't want your money," Avis spat at her. "I don't want anything from you, Betsey Smith. I've seen you and now I know. I was better off in that hell as an orphan than being your daughter. I'm going back to Denver soon. I don't want to stay here and shame you. Good day."

Something, Avis never knew what, swept her out of that horrible room with the huge bed.

She slowly descended the staircase and when she reached the bottom, made eye contact with Liam who awaited her in the parlor. And collapsed.

CHAPTER THIRTEEN

Liam carried Avis's limp body to one of the davenports in the saloon. "What happened to her?"

Angelique came to him and hovered around looking concerned.

"You get the doctor." No. That wouldn't do.

Angelique held out a slim finger and raced from the room. Boum Boum and Jolie clutched each other in fright. Until a miner came in the door, then they turned from Avis and Liam and turned on their charms in the hopes of getting the miner's money.

Angelique came back with a smelling salt and the Madam. "What happened?" Madam's shrill voice rose in desperation. "She can't do that in here."

"Where would be a good place for you, Madame Bonheur, given the kind of shock she has had?" Liam broke the smelling salt under Avis's nose, gently waving around the contents.

The three of them watched Avis come to. She tried to sit up as her eyes opened. "Easy. Take it easy." Madam's voice rang with something that sounded like care and concern.

Liam was not sure, though. "I'll take her out of here. Thank you for your couch for a few minutes."

"There's no need to be terse with me, Fulton."

"I think you know why I'm being terse with you. You might have been kind."

"She told you?"

"Yes, she did."

Madam looked around the parlor. Angelique's eyes went wide as she stared at the madam. "Well, don't look at me. She's crazy."

"You mean she's wrong?"

Madam shrugged and pulled her shawl around her to better emphasize her big bosom. Liam wasn't fooled. "Smith is a very common name. She could be anyone."

"You know exactly who she is. Given what happened yesterday and today, she's better off without you in her life." Liam lifted Avis's delicate body into his arms. "Angelique, if you could get the door, I'll take Miss Smith out of here."

Avis fit perfectly in his arms. The cold air of the outside swirled around them, and she shook her hair. Her lovely curls blew free in the wind. "What... What are you doing, Mr. Fulton?"

"You've had quite a shock. I don't think you should work today. You get a day off."

Angelique knocked in a hurried way on the heavy oak door of La Maison. Arabella opened the door. "What happened to her?" Liam pushed past the obnoxious blonde and carried Avis into the parlor, calling for Milly.

Milly came hurrying out and when she saw Avis in Liam's arms, patted on Avis's limbs. "Her hands are so cold. Wrap her in a blanket. "

Angelique left, especially because it was clear that Arabella was going to stand there and stare at everyone.

"Miss Smith has had a huge shock. I brought her back home. She needs a day off."

"You've been over there working her like a slave. She needs some time. Trying to get your measure of labor from this girl."

Liam's heart sank. "I could never repay Miss Smith for all she's done for me."

Avis patted his hand. "Thank you, Mr. Fulton. You've been extremely kind to me. I appreciate all you have done."

Liam put his hand over hers and grasped it. Milly was right. Her hand was cold. Something compelled him to put her cold hands between his warm ones to help her. "Maybe some coffee would help you."

"I'll be alright. I just need to rest myself. I've pushed myself too hard, and I haven't been properly nourished yet." Avis looked at Liam. "I'll be at the store before you know it."

"I told her she could have a day off."

"A good idea, Liam. You can be over here and hold her hands all day if you like." Milly suggested.

Liam let go of Avis's soft hands.

"You need to go back to the store. I'll be fine here."

"You sure?"

"Yes." Avis grasped his hand, and her hand did seem warmer now. "Thank you, Mr. Fulton."

"I'll come back after I've waited on them."

"Go open the store. I'll be fine."

Seeing Milly there with a cup of hot coffee, he stood and brought the coffee around to Avis. Now her hands would be warm. She smiled at him and brushed him away with a gesture. He left, but as he exited La Maison, he wondered what it was that Madam had said to Avis. Madam was a cold, calculating woman to chase such a worthy woman away from her.

He opened the store and, for the rest of the morning, did brisk business with some of the miners.

When things slowed down, he went to his law books to see what the law said regarding the fate of a young woman like Avis Smith. Could JD Jones be right?

He looked through three books until he found what he was looking for. Except for the small part of Colorado remanded from Mexico, marriage between a white person and a colored or mulatto person was illegal in the territory and now the state. Noelle was not in that part of Colorado, it was too far north.

Something inside of him burned. Why would such an unjust law be passed in the territory? He knew. Colorado was a state with enormous promise. White people didn't want the formerly enslaved to come to the state. From its territorial founding, Colorado was supposed to be a slave holding territory and in other places where slave ownership was a possibility, no marriages were permitted between owners and slaves. When Colorado was granted statehood earlier in the year, Liam knew the lawmakers saw no reason to overturn the law. Such a law would discourage colored people of any stripe to settle there and there would be more land for white people in the state, except for that one thin strip, south of them. Because it had belonged to Mexico, that was different. His family had history here in the United States going back nearly three hundred years and in England, a few more hundred before that. Still, he had never felt such shame in his heritage as he did now. That someone else's greed could manifest itself in preventing his happiness and the town of Noelle from being settled seemed abhorrent. How in the world could he make this right? How could he help Avis, Miss Smith, find a happy ending? Her skills, her gifts, her energy all belonged here in Noelle. He knew that much.

Marriage. That's what the brides were here for. He had paid for her train fare. He could also marry JD's bride.

Something warmed in him at the possibility. Would Avis want to marry him? He was old enough to be her father. Well, not quite, but some years older than her. Would she want him?

She had cleared out the upper apartment of the store nearly single-handed. The upstairs could be a home. Later, he could buy a piece of land, and they could settle on it. She would be a wonderful partner to run the store as he studied and began a young law practice here. They could work together, side by side, and provide very important services to the town. If it weren't for some stupid unjust law passed by a bigoted territorial legislature.

A walk might help him figure it out. Then he could go check on Avis. He closed the store and went down to La Maison. Milly told him Avis was upstairs resting. She offered him a bowl of stew for dinner, but he wasn't hungry. His mind was consumed with this problem and a walk in the snow might help him clear his head.

West of Noelle there was a lake, and it often occurred to him that it would be a nice place to live. There would be several varieties of birds that would come there, and they could watch them together. Something about the thought of a springtime with Avis cheered him, if only she would have him. It seemed like a small foolish wish. How could he make it happen?

Then, as he watched the wind whip on the grasses by the pond, an idea occurred to him. It would probably take all of the money he had saved. Still, if he were able to use it, his future and by extension Avis's future would be secure. He thought of the way her hair looked, tossed all around her lovely heart-shaped face. She was someone who deserved comfort and care. He could provide that for her, if she would have it.

He knelt in the snow and prayed. *Lord, give me strength and purpose to see to helping Miss Smith. She's someone who has lived too much of a rough life, and she deserves better than the rotten hand life has dealt her. Let me help her. Let me protect her. In your name, Jesus. Amen.*

The prayer made him feel better. He walked back into town, ready to open the store and maybe to see Avis later in the evening. What would he say to her to convince her that this plan was what needed to happen to help her? He needed to be more eloquent in order to pull off the life of a lawyer. He would let his heart speak for him.

As he came into town, he saw Doc Deane get down from a carriage in a hurry and go into the abandoned saloon where Madam and her girls were staying. "Something happen?" Liam called out.

"Some of these rough riders came through town and beat up one of Madam's girls. I'm checking on her." Doc Deane stopped and regarded him.

"I think it's the one you like."

"Angelique?" Liam stepped forward and through the door with the doctor.

"Yea, the mulatta one."

"She's just a kid."

"I agree. And that Madam, she must be something to work for. I wouldn't want to tangle with her."

No. No one should.

No one. Not even Avis, his future wife.

The two men walked through the doors of the saloon to see Angelique holding a wadded ball of cloth to her head, laying on the same davenport where Avis had been just a few hours ago. His mind flashed back to his deceased fiancée. Did his care bring devastation to every woman he had ever loved?

CHAPTER FOURTEEN
The Sixth Day of Christmas-- December 30, 1876

When Avis woke the next morning, she ached to see Mr. Fulton. There was so much to tell her new friend about her face to face confrontation with Betsey Smith. The woman's cavalier attitude and her shock at her skin tone was not what Avis had expected.

Still, when she went downstairs everyone was in a furor about the prostitute Pearl marrying the sheriff the day before. "Five weddings. That's well on the road to helping Noelle!" Penny proclaimed.

"I wonder who will be next." Minnie leaned forward, helping herself to a slice of toasted bread.

"It will probably be me," Arabella purred. "I've known Hugh for so long. Our marriage is a fait a'compli." They all rolled their eyes. How unfortunate that they thought they were getting rid of Maybelle and she came back resurrected in the even more insufferable form of Arabella.

Avis stood. "I'm ready to report for duty. Mr. Fulton doesn't need a lazy bones lying around. I'm going to get my breakfast and get right to Cobb's Penn."

Milly came in with a plate heaped with eggs, bacon, sausage patties, hash brown potatoes and two biscuits struggling to stay on the plate full of food. She glared at Avis who sat back down. "Eat this hot breakfast, Miss Smith. Mr. Fulton left a note with me for you. But first, eat up and then you get your note."

The other ladies smiled at Milly. "Are you trying to catch a man or a cow with that plate?" Arabella's eyes crossed at the plate full of food.

"Avis can afford it," Minnie told her in a tone that let Arabella know she could not. "Go on, Avis. Eat. We can't wait to see what Mr. Fulton said to you."

"Maybe you'll be next." Penny suggested. "He was ever so kind when I knocked down the display in the store a few days ago. I think he has a soft spot for the brides."

"No, Penny. Just one." Minnie elbowed her, and they both grinned at Avis.

"Mr. Fulton is kind to everyone. I think that is his most singular characteristic." She informed them. Still, it crossed Avis's mind that there would be people Liam was not or could not be as kind to, and she shuddered thinking of JD Jones.

"Ahh yes, Right. Nonetheless, I think I'll let Birdie know a thing or two about you needing a dress soon." Penny cupped her lips, whispering to Avis.

"I'm going back to Denver. I don't think that will happen."

Their breakfasts finished, Minnie and Penny stood and went into the parlor, arms linked, continuing to plot.

Did Mr. Fulton feel that way about her? His constant regard for her was nothing but genteel manners. It was the very quality that would make him a perfect lawyer for Noelle. It had nothing to do with her. But then, she recalled the way he touched her, the care with which he had carried her, and the look of longing in his face when she awakened from her episode yesterday. Her heart palpitated a bit, but she squelched it. There was nothing here for her in Noelle. That was her reality. Nothing else.

Maybe the note would explain why he wasn't here this morning. She didn't want to walk across the street alone, although she would if she had to.

Miss Smith:

Please take the morning to have a care for yourself. I believe I have come up with a solution to your situation with Madame Bonheur, and I will need the morning to tie up a few loose ends. I will be by for you at midday. Milly promises to fix a nice meal, and then we will depart for Cobb's Penn for the rest of the day. Saturday is usually a busy day at the store because people drive in to replenish stock, but these are important matters. When you have a moment, pray for me. I know the moment the words leave your lips, your caring for me will enter my soul and I will be well supported.

Your protector,
William C. Fulton

He had quite a way with words. The beauty of what he had written swirled about in her heart and mind, and she was not quite sure of what she should do. Milly came in, loudly proclaiming that she better finish her plate.

"I'm to wait here until he comes?"

"That's what Mr. Fulton said. And you will do it, even if I have to sit on you myself." The sizable woman gave a hearty laugh. Avis laughed too.

"Well, it has been some time since I've caught up on my knitting. I can do that."

"Yes, in the parlor. You go right in there and make yourself comfortable. I'm building a stew for dinner."

Avis retrieved her yarn ends and pulled up a chair that faced the main street. It did feel nice to relax and see what was going on in Noelle on a busy Saturday morning. She could look out on the activity, be productive, and wonder.

She saw Mr. Fulton ride by on a horse headed west out of town. He turned toward the house and waved at her. She waved back. He wore his hunting jacket and denim, and that uncontrollable red hair of his stuck out beneath a woolen hunter cap as he rode away. She didn't know the layout of the town that well. All she could do was knit and wait.

What was Mr. Fulton up to?

She didn't know, but she bowed her head and prayed for him, as he asked her to do.

Given all that Avis had told him about her childhood, he knew she had never had the opportunity to celebrate her birthday. Now, he had the opportunity to give her the gifts that she wanted the most: for JD Jones to leave her alone and for Madam Bonheur to show some shred of motherly feeling for her. It struck him that these two desires of Avis's heart kept it caged and kept her from believing herself worthy of happiness. If he could resolve these problems, then she would be free. That was all he wanted for her. His admiration was so deep he would be fine living life without her if he knew she would be happy and free of her woes.

First, he would seek out Jones in the miner's housing on the outskirts of town. He went to rent out a horse from Culver Daniels. Liam couldn't help but notice that the men of Noelle were looking mighty chipper these days. Culver loaned him a pony, and Liam watched him go back into his house with his lovely new bride, Kezia waving over Culver's shoulder at him. He heard the squeal and laughter of a baby and then the door shut, keeping him and the world out.

Completely unaware of the cold, Liam rode on for about thirty minutes until he pulled the pony up to the wooden longhouse where the miners lived. Liam walked up to the front door and knocked on it. He was greeted by Tom pulling up his suspenders, getting ready for the day. "Where's Jones?"

Tom's eyebrows went mountain high. Liam's enmity for Jones was no secret. "He's over there in bed. Still hungover, I guess."

No surprises there. He stepped into the longhouse, which reeked of smoke and unwashed men, and went in the direction of Jones's lower bunk. Watching the man sleep, who had caused many so much trouble, almost made his stomach turn. But, Liam had work to do to see to the happiness of the young woman he had come to love in such a short amount of time. He kicked JD with his boot. "Jones, get up."

JD sat up so fast he hit his head on the timbers above him. Some of the miners laughed at the sound of his bald head meeting the wood above him. "What do you want, Fulton?"

"Get up and get dressed. I want to talk to you for a minute."

"I've got nothing to say to you."

Liam reached down and grabbed Jones by his long john shirt. He pulled the man out of his bunk. "I asked nicely." He said, dumping Jones on the floor.

"Hey! You've got no right to do that."

Liam noticed all of the other miners were looking the other way. Not one of them rose to defend Jones or ask Liam what he was doing. A clear indication of how they felt about the man. "I'll be outside. I'm giving you five minutes. If you aren't out there, I'm coming back in here to get you."

Liam strode out of the longhouse and picked up snow rubbing it all over his hands to get the filth of Jones off of him. He should have worn gloves.

JD Jones came out in a few minutes. "What do you want?"

Liam pulled a package out of his pocket. "This envelope has one thousand dollars in it. I want you to take it. I have written off your tab as well. Take this money and get out of Noelle. If you come back, I'll kill you myself."

Jones gave him an evil grin. "You must want my bride, Fulton. Fancy that."

"I do. And I want you to keep silent."

"About her heritage? Oh, I would never dream——"

Liam grabbed him again. This time, he lifted Jones off the ground and threw him into the snow. "Hey, what was that for?"

"To show you I meant what I said. What do you want to do? This money is more than you'll ever make prospecting up here. Take it and go away."

The man's beady eyes grew large. "Yes, give it to me."

Liam threw the leatherwork pouch that Grandpa Gus had made for him onto Jones. It bounced off his forehead, and watching the man scramble, Liam nearly wanted to laugh at how he dug for the money. "Never come near her again. Never."

"Fine. Okay." Jones opened the pouch and thumbed through the money. "I'm gone today."

"Now. Leave right now."

"As you say, Fulton. Thanks!"

Liam picked up more snow and rubbed it between his hands before getting on the pony again. One problem solved. Now for the next one.

He rode the pony to the abandoned saloon and went in with a swagger. All of the girls were sitting around waiting for their Saturday morning traffic to come. Angelique stood, waving her hands. "I'm going up there, Angelique. None of you can stop me."

"Hey," Jolie kicked a lazy leg out, "if we had a new Madam, things might be better around here. First door on the right."

None of them stopped him. Liam took the steps two at a time and knocked on the shut door.

"I'm not seeing anyone, Jolie."

"Open the door, Madam Bonheur."

There was rustling behind the door, then the door to her room swung open. She was truly a sight. It was clear to Liam she had been crying. Did Madam care about Avis? Would this be easier than he thought?

"What do you want?"

Liam pushed past her. "Tomorrow is Avis's birthday."

"You think I don't know that?"

"I'm giving her a party after the church service. I want you to come."

Madam laughed. "If I stepped foot in that service, Hammond would have a fit."

"You can come at the end. This is what I want you to give her."

Madam held up a hand. "You're in no position to tell me what to do."

Liam shook his head. "Actually, I am. I'm going to ask her to marry me."

"You are?" Madam's tired, red-rimmed eyes grew wide.

"I am. I've fallen in love with her. I want her to have a family and love for always. I want to give that to her on her birthday, if she will have me."

Madam whipped out a crumpled hanky. "Oh, that's so wonderful. Just like Jamie. He would talk wonderful like that to me too."

"Are you willing to do what I say?"

"If you think it will help."

"It will. Sit down while I explain."

Betsey Smith sat on a wooden chair and, for the first time in her tortured life, actually listened to someone.

CHAPTER FIFTEEN
The Seventh Day —December 31, 1876

Avis was a little surprised when Mr. Fulton asked her to go to the church service at The Golden Nugget on their walk back to La Maison.

She had several thoughts, one of them being that it was her birthday and it might be nice to sleep in for a change. Then, she thought about how her life had changed over the past week. Noelle had become a place where she felt as if she might belong. All of the people who welcomed her, gave her respect, nourished and fed her would be worshipping there at The Golden Nugget. That's where she wanted to be.

"Yes, I'll come."

Mr. Fulton patted her hand.

This time, instead of letting go of her fingertips, he grasped them and planted a warm, lingering kiss on the backside of her hand.

"What, what was that for?" Avis's frosty breath rushed out of her all at once.

"A thank you, Miss Smith. For giving God a chance on your birthday. I'll be here for you at eight."

He turned and walked away. She enjoyed watching him stride away. Even in the snow, his gait stayed even.

Avis neared the door and noticed a few of the brides hovering in the window, waving at the two of them. She shook her head and laughed. The giggles felt like bubbles inside of her. She didn't even remember to look over at the abandoned saloon.

She wanted to see if Molly would show up at the service. Everyone had been abuzz about her wedding. Half of the brides were married up. Noelle was just about halfway there.

Her black dress had been dried and clean and she donned it, making sure her hair was extra smooth.

Just as she arrived at breakfast where Milly was serving flapjacks with bacon and hot coffee, Liam entered the parlor. His eyes went wide looking at her. "You look well rested, Miss Smith."

"Thank you, Mr. Fulton." She didn't know why she should feel embarrassed at the hand kissing last night, but she did.

Liam generously agreed to walk all of the brides, or the ones that were left, to the church service. Future brides met new brides and their husbands, lending the saloon a more festive air for the service.

Reverend Hammond spoke well of the prospects of Noelle. "When Charlie comes out of the mountains, he will see the astounding success we have had. Surely, we will triumph and get the railroad in here." He nodded to Percival Penworthy, whose face was scrunched up in a smug look.

Reverend Hammond gave the benediction, and everyone helped Seamus rearrange the tables in the saloon. Avis stood to the side, talking with Fina about the restaurant and what she was learning to cook. Avis needed to learn herself. She had a completely different attitude now. Cooking was about making sure she was properly nourished, something that was a possibility.

"Are we leaving soon, Mr. Fulton?" She called out to him as he swept past her, sleeves rolled up as he helped rearrange the room.

"In a while," he said.

All of the brides remained in the saloon with a few others, and Avis watched Birdie lay white cloths on some of the tables. That wasn't the usual set up for the saloon. What was going on?

"What are those white cloths for?"

"Chica, I have no idea." Fina said rather loudly.

Avis knew she was lying. She had done it a little too often herself not to know the signs, but why?

All of a sudden, Seamus came out of the back of the saloon carrying a cake.

"Happy Birthday, Avis!" Everyone screamed.

Her birthday. Only two people in the town knew it was her birthday. Mr. Fulton remembered. That was so kind of him. Everyone sang a chorus of *For He's a Jolly Good Fellow* to her, and Mr. Fulton wrapped his arm around her, enveloping her in a semi-embrace. "Do you like your surprise, Miss Smith?"

Avis looked at him with tears in her eyes. "I do. I've never felt so, so included. Thank you. Thank you, everyone."

The entire room clapped.

"There's one more thing, Miss Smith." The entire room hushed. "You've changed lives since you arrived in Noelle. This is a better town and a better place because you are here. I know we made an agreement a week ago to have you earn money to go back to Denver. But things have changed. I have changed."

He turned to her. "Miss Avis Smith, I've fallen in love with you. Would you do me the honor of becoming my wife?"

There it was. Words she never thought would be spoken to her were in the air. Mr. Fulton, Liam, was speaking the kind, wonderful words of love to her, and even more, he wanted her to be his wife. But, it could never be.

"Oh, Mr. Fulton. I'm so honored."

Liam looked down at her. "Are you going to say no?"

"I can't. It's not possible." Avis lowered her head, feeling the most overwhelming rejection. Liam's kind, blue eyes bore traces of hurt. "I've fallen in love with you as well, Liam. But my heritage. I… I…cannot."

A pall had fallen over the whole room. "I want to help Noelle, I do. But I would not bring shame on it either."

Liam nodded his head. He didn't look upset at her refusal. Not as upset as she thought he would. "Would you permit me, Miss Smith, the honor of one more guest to your birthday party?"

He stepped out onto the porch of the saloon.

"What in tarnation is going on?" Grandpa Gus broke the silence. Everyone murmured to themselves.

Avis didn't know. She looked in the direction of the door where Liam had disappeared and saw him pull Madam into the room. There were audible gasps, especially from Birdie — for understandable reasons.

"Go ahead." Liam elbowed Madam. He rejoined Avis and put a fortifying arm around her.

Avis looked at Betsey Smith, who was modestly dressed, for once, in a dark lavender lace creation.

"I'm not here to ruin anyone's good time. I just wanted to say Happy Birthday. I'll be leaving soon."

"Good. Say it and go." Birdie shouted at her.

"I've got something to say." Madam gathered her shawl about herself. "And, I'm gonna say it."

People in the room quieted.

"What do you have to say?" Avis half wished she would go as Birdie desired.

"Twenty-one years ago today, in New Hampshire, I gave birth to a girl. A beautiful baby girl. I named her Avis."

The room erupted in shocked murmurs and whispers, but Avis was still.

Why was she doing this?

"Happy Birthday, Avis Elizabeth. I'm sorry if I caused you pain in your life. I hope you enjoy your day and please, one day I hope you will find it in your heart to forgive me. Once you marry Mr. Fulton, I know he'll take good care of you and any children you might bring into the world. But, I won't ever disgrace them. You won't have to worry about that."

Tears welled up in her eyes. This was a birthday gift of a kind. One that she could accept.

"Hold on just a minute." A male voice rung out from the back of the room. The brides, and some of the grooms, parted as Percival stepped forward. "There can be no marriage with you, Fulton. She's part colored, isn't she?"

"I have no idea what you are doing at this party, Percival." Liam's voice was as cool as the Colorado Rockies. He slid his hand down to Avis's waist, and she liked the feel of his hand there. "You weren't invited."

"Maybe not, but I'm not going to stand by and let this happen. It won't count."

Liam patted Avis's hip. She was not faint at all. It was as if she had an armor on in his embrace. Nothing would hurt her. Not Percival or JD Jones. "You said she's colored. Well, we have her mother right here. We can see she's not, right?"

Percival nodded.

"Well, Madam. Is Avis part Negro?"

The entire room swung to where Madam was standing. Avis's eyes met her mother's. Madam drew herself up. "She is my daughter. I'm a whore. I have no idea who her father was."

The tears that had threatened to spill onto Avis's cheeks fell unbidden. Percival held up his hands. "There is a law that says coloreds and mulatto people cannot marry whites in Colorado. It's been in existence for thirty years. That's why we had to make sure the brides were who they were. It's a law."

Chase Hammond stepped forward. "It's a terrible law. I had heard talk from Denver of doing away with it."

"Regardless, it's the law." Percival stomped his foot.

Liam eyed the man. "So how do you prove that someone is colored or mulatta in Colorado?"

Percival backed down. "I don't know."

"Let me tell you. People have to witness a sworn testimony by parties that know of the heritage of said person. That's how." Liam informed him, and a buzz went around the room.

Chase's eyes were focused on them both. "That just happened, Percival. Madam is her mother. She would know. She just said she doesn't know who Avis's father is."

Betsey Smith nodded. "Yes, my clientele is white with the occasional Mexican. Always has been."

"There you are," Liam said. "She just said a white man was her father."

"That's right." Madam drew herself up.

"She's a whore. Are we going to believe her?" Percival folded his arms.

"Who do you think we should believe? She's her mother." Liam fixed his gaze on Percival.

Everyone waited to see his reaction. Percival turned on his heel and left. A cheer went up in the room.

Liam and Avis embraced one another. "Will you marry me?" Liam whispered into her ear.

"Yes, I will, Mr. Fulton."

He pulled her back from him. "Really?"

Avis nodded her head. "Yes, really."

"When?"

She looked all around the room at the faces looking at her. Acceptance. She had finally found a place where she belonged. It would never be better than this. "Right now. Yes, right now."

"I do." Liam said, and they went towards each other for a kiss. His kiss, featherlight on her lips, caused all of the doubt and rejection to melt away from her. Liam's kiss had transformed her from the vengeful Avis she had been when she came to Noelle.

When they broke apart, several of the men congratulated Liam. "You'll only have one day to remember. The last day of the year!"

"Wait, you cannot get married in black. It just cannot be." Small Birdie Peregrine burst out. Everyone laughed, and Jack put an arm around his bride. "No, I mean it." Birdie held out a hand. "Come with me, Avis. I have something in my house."

"Oh my, I…" Avis allowed herself to be pulled along. Fina and Penny went behind her as well.

"I have just the thing," Birdie declared.

"What is it?"

Birdie pulled them into the place where she kept her fabrics and her partially made up dresses. She pulled one out from behind the others. It was a dress made of white.

They oohed and ahhed. "This can't be what you meant. I've never had anything so beautiful."

"This is exactly what I mean, swan bird. I'm going to fit this to you. Now, get that black gown off of her."

"This is perfect for you, chica."

"Yes, it is."

"It's so fine," Avis protested.

"Nonsense. You are going to be Mrs. Fulton. Everyone knows you have been running that shop, and given that piece of lawyering your future husband just did, you're going to be the wife of a great lawyer too!" Birdie helped her out of the black dress as she spoke.

She was right. Reassuring Penny they did not need her help, Fina and Birdie fit the gown to her. In thirty minutes, they helped Avis back across the street in her new, fine white bridal dress. The entire saloon oohed and ahhed as she entered. Liam stood next to Chase Hammond as she walked to him, her eyes only on him as she became Mrs. William Cobb Fulton.

Finally, she was accepted in the heart of the town of Noelle. Rejection was a thing of the past.

EPILOGUE
Later that night

Later that night, Liam pulled out his pocket watch as he watched his bride brush her bounteous hair while sitting crossed legged on their large bed in their new upstairs living quarters above Cobb's Penn. His bride's exclamation stopped him from opening it up to view the time.

"You're an amazing man, Mr. Fulton."

"Thank you, Mrs. Fulton. No more amazing than you are."

"I'll never know how you managed to do all of this." She spread her arms to indicate the fully furnished space, complete with rugs on the floor, a large bed covered with quilts, a wardrobe, nightstands, and a vanity.

"It was your idea, my dear. You said I should live up here, and I do now... with you. It's our little nest, for now."

She smiled at him. "I can't believe it's the same space I cleared out just a few days ago." His bride's brow furrowed. "Did you see the tree before we left the saloon?"

"The tree?"

"Yes, the Christmas tree. It's getting more and more decorated as the days go by. I noticed a pair of swans on the tree."

"Really?"

"Yes, they made a heart. That's how I saw them. I saw a heart on the tree and I stared at them. A pair of swans. Male and female."

"Did they look like they were very much in love swan birds?"

Avis slid herself down on him and nestled in the crook of her husband's bare arm, positioning herself comfortably against his well-muscled, bare chest. "Why, yes, they were."

She reached up to kiss him, but her husband pointed to his pocket watch and opened it so they could both see the time. "Ahh, Happy 1877, Mrs. Fulton."

"Happy New Year to you, Mr. Fulton." Avis leaned into him, her lips upraised to his, ready to finish what she had started.

And the two of them, cob and pen, celebrated.

THE END

AUTHOR'S NOTE

I hope that you enjoyed Avis and Liam's love story. It was a proud day for me when Caroline Lee asked me to be part of this group of authors. You see, I was super jealous when the America's Mail-Order Bride series was released two years ago. Fortunately, I met the right people, joined the right groups and there I was, in May 2017, attending a group meeting at the Romantic Times convention with other authors to discuss this amazing idea.

Still, when I entered the meeting space, I had concerns. Would I be welcome? Would the way I write history be welcome? I had written historical romance before, but not western ones. I was pleased to see that I was greeted with enthusiasm. During the meeting, it occurred to me that if I were to be part of this collection, my story would be one that asked that same question: Would Noelle welcome all different kinds of people?

Some people don't approve of discussion of the unpleasant moments in United States history. I understand that. However, from my perspective, the topic has to be brought up, addressed, and dealt with if we don't want that awful history to be repeated. The unpleasantness of the west isn't widely discussed. I learned, just a few years ago, about the laws enacted to keep African Americans away from certain western states. When I did learn about it, I knew that I would have to write that history one day. So when I left that hotel room meeting, I knew that this series would be my chance to write about the unpleasant history of Colorado, a state where my beloved sister resides right now.

The law against interracial marriage between whites and blacks or mulattos was real, and it remained in place until 1957—just ten years before the Supreme Court dealt with the issue. Colorado is strange because there was one thin strip on the southwest side where interracial marriage was always permitted, but not in the rest of the state. I toyed with having Avis and Liam go there in some way, but that did Noelle no good. It also didn't answer the question that mattered most to me: What kind of town was Noelle going to be?

I'm glad that I figured out the answer. While I'm not the typical western writer, I hope that you were rooting for Avis and you could see Liam for the great protector he was. That's what cob swans do, after all! Cygnets are not that attractive at the beginning of their lives, but with patience, in time, they transform into beautiful cob and pen swans who mate for life.

If you are interested in the history of African Americans in the West I recommend these books:

African American Women of the Old West by Tricia Wagoner
In Search of the Racial Frontier: African Americans in the West 1528-1990 by Quintard Taylor

BOOKS BY PIPER HUGULEY

The Lawyer's Luck – Available on Amazon, Print (CreateSpace), Barnes and Noble and Kobo

Amazon: http://www.amazon.com/Lawyers-Luck-Milford-College-prequel-ebook/dp/B00LBIKE38/ref=sr_1_1?s=digital-text&ie=UTF8&qid=1419615151&sr=1-1&keywords=the+lawyer%27s+luck

CreateSpace: http://www.amazon.com/The-Lawyers-Luck-Milford-College/dp/0692248536/ref=tmm_pap_title_0?ie=UTF8&qid=1419615151&sr=1-1

Barnes and Noble: http://www.barnesandnoble.com/w/the-lawyers-luck-piper-huguley/1119878710?ean=2940149726448

Kobo: http://store.kobobooks.com/en-US/ebook/the-lawyer-s-luck

The Preacher's Promise – Available on Amazon and in print

Amazon ebook: http://www.amazon.com/Preachers-Promise-Home-Milford-College-ebook/dp/B00M77K09U/ref=tmm_kin_swatch_0?_encoding=UTF8&sr=&qid=

CreateSpace: http://www.amazon.com/The-Preachers-Promise-Milford-College/dp/1500851914/ref=pd_bxgy_b_img_y

Barnes and Noble: http://www.barnesandnoble.com/w/the-preachers-promise-piper-huguley/1120019525?ean=2940149661411

The Mayor's Mission- Available on Amazon and Nook:

Amazon ebook: http://www.amazon.com/Mayors-Mission-Home-Milford-College-ebook/dp/B00RGVPM9A/ref=sr_1_4?s=digital-text&ie=UTF8&qid=1419612349&sr=1-4&keywords=piper+huguley

Barnes and Noble (Paperback): http://www.barnesandnoble.com/w/the-mayors-mission-piper-huguley/1120968964?ean=9781512269628

The Representative's Revolt—Available on Amazon and Nook

Amazon e-book: https://www.amazon.com/Representatives-Revolt-Milford-College-novel-ebook/dp/B019YN8BS6
Nook: https://www.barnesandnoble.com/w/the-representatives-revolt-piper-huguley/1124222556?ean=2940156886401

A Champion's Heart—available only on Amazon and in print
Amazon e-book: https://www.amazon.com/Champions-Heart-Born-Win-Men-ebook/dp/B01LYB0LPD
CreateSpace: https://www.amazon.com/Champions-Heart-Born-Win-Men/dp/1541215125/

WHAT'S NEXT
The Maid
The Eighth Day

Summer, Denver 1876

"Easy knowing the nuns trained you, child. I can see me own face in those pots."

Cara blushed with pride at Cook's comment although her knuckles were raw from scrubbing.

When she had first arrived at the Benevolent Society of Lost Lambs, Cook had initially dismissed her as yet another society girl who wanted to while away a few hours of the day. But as the weeks passed, she'd changed her mind.

"Cara, there is someone here to see you. Can you change and come to the drawing room please?"

"Yes, Mrs. Walters." Cara handed back the oven cloths to Cook.

"Maybe it's your family, Cara?"

"Doubt it, Cook. As far as my mama is concerned, I'm dead."

She walked quickly upstairs wondering who was waiting for her. Nobody from Boston knew where she was. Sister Maura wouldn't tell. Maybe Mrs. Walters had found her a nursing position. She dressed carefully, tucking her hair back off her face. She checked her hands and nails; they were clean but a little rough. They didn't expect real nurses to have soft, creamy, milk-colored hands, did they?

Cara took the stairs carefully hoping to present an image of a well brought up, young, intelligent woman who knew her own mind. Taking a deep breath, she knocked at the door. Mrs. Walters called her to come in.

Cara opened the door and nearly fainted. Sitting there grinning like a Cheshire cat was the man who dominated all her nightmares. Senator Kavanagh.

"What are you doing here?"

"Now, Miss O'Donnell, where are your manners? That is not the way to greet your fiancé is it?" He said, staring at her with an expression of distaste.

"My what? I didn't agree to marry you."

"Your intended says your parents have given consent, Cara," Mrs. Walters

95

interjected.

"No. I can't. I won't." Cara insisted, fisting her hands at either side of her body.

A scream interrupted them. "Excuse me, sounds like the new girl has burnt herself. Again. I know it's not proper to leave you without a chaperone, but I will leave the door open. Mr. Kavanagh will behave like a gentleman." Mrs. Walters gave Mr. Kavanagh a piercing look, and he nodded.

Cara turned to go with Mrs. Walters, but Senator Kavanagh was too quick for her. Despite his size and age, he maneuvered himself between her and her protector.

"My dear, Miss O'Donnell, how I have missed you. I was so worried when you left Boston, I spared no expense in tracking you down. You can't hide from me, my darling."

Anyone listening in the hall would assume these were words of love from a lovesick suitor. Only Cara saw the malevolent look in his eyes. A veneer of decency masked the cruelty she sensed. She took a step backwards. It was a mistake, as she stumbled and ended up sitting on the sofa. He sat beside her, pinning her to the chair with the weight of his body. Her hand held firmly in his hand.

"Cara, I mean to have you. I have offered marriage, but one way or another, I will own you. You're wise to cease making a spectacle of yourself and your family. Agree to return with me today."

"Never!"

"You will do as I bid. Otherwise, your dear mama has agreed to admit you to the lunatic asylum."

"She wouldn't, she couldn't. Papa wouldn't allow it."

"I think we both know who controls your parents' household, Miss O'Donnell. Now, my darling, just name the date. I have waited so long. I cannot wait any longer."

Panicked, Cara looked around for an escape. He moved closer as if sensing her desire to flee. Her heartbeat was too fast for her to breathe properly. Her stays sticking into her flesh. His noxious breath wafting under her nostrils, sweaty palm affixed to hers. She couldn't move, couldn't breathe. She opened her mouth to scream.

"Sorry about that, Senator Kavanagh, Cara. Poor Sandra, she is far too clumsy in the kitchen. Cook wants me to give her notice and replace her with Cara."

"Out of the question Mrs. Walters. My fiancé is a not a charwoman. Now, darling, please go and pack. I have tickets for the train back to Boston leaving this evening."

"Cara couldn't possibly be ready to leave this afternoon. She has commitments which must be honored, including dinner with a very prominent member of Denver society." Mrs. Walters spoke in a very decisive tone. Cara had rarely heard her use it, but when she did, nobody argued. "She will be ready to leave three days from now."

"But…" For the first time Senator Kavanagh looked a little unsure of himself.

"Oh, is that the time? Excuse me, Senator, but Cara and I have plans for this afternoon. Perhaps you could call back on Thursday? It was so lovely to meet you." Mrs. Walker dismissed him, helping Cara off of the sofa where she was still pinned by his body. "Cara, could you fetch the Senator's coat? Thank you."

Cara didn't need asking twice. She fetched his coat, more or less threw it at him and disappeared upstairs. Mrs. Walters would have to deal with him, but she sensed the lady was stronger than she looked.

***

Mrs. Walters pushed the door of the Cara's room open.

"Cara, dear don't cry. You will ruin your face. He's not worth it."

"Did you hear what he said?"

"About the asylum? Yes, dear. But, surely your parents…"

"They would. He's right. Mama can make Papa do whatever she wishes. She hates me."

"But why?"

"I wasn't born a boy."

Mrs. Walters opened her arms, and Cara fell into her embrace. She cried until she had no tears left. Mrs. Walters didn't make any attempt to stop her. When the tears were gone, and she sniffed quietly, or at least tried to, Mrs. Walters gave her a hanky.

"Cara, are you over twenty-one?"

"Yes, Mrs. Walters. It was my birthday yesterday."

"I believe I have a solution to your problem. You will have to make a difficult decision but at least it will be your choice. People will say I should probably not get involved, but I simply cannot stand by and watch a lovely young girl be bullied into marriage to a self-opinionated old goat like that man."

"Oh, Mrs. Walters, can you really help me?"

"I can help you help yourself, Cara." Mrs. Walters clarified.

Cara sat and listened in amazement as Mrs. Walters outlined her plan. Cara would become a mail order bride. Having a husband was the only thing that would protect her from both her mama and the Senator.

First, she would have to pretend to run away but go into hiding instead. They needed Senator Kavanagh to go back to Boston. Mrs. Walters knew a hospital, which would offer her sanctuary in return for some help on the wards.

"It will involve a lot of back breaking scrubbing, Cara, not to mention unpleasant encounters with various illnesses."

"I am strong and healthy, and if I get sick of it I will only have to think of his face."

Mrs. Walters patted her hand. "You will need to write a letter to your intended. I have a letter from a doctor. Seems to be a match made in heaven given you want to nurse."

"Is he kind? Young?"

"Good heavens, girl. I haven't met him." Mrs. Walters softened her tone. "I assume so from what he tells me… assuming he is being honest."

"He can't be any worse than the Senator, can he?"

Mrs. Walters appeared to hesitate, but Cara told herself she was imagining it. "There will be eleven other brides. I will accompany you all to Noelle, a small town in the Colorado mountains."

"Perfect for hiding from Kavanagh. No one would think to look for me there. Oh, Mrs. Walters, I think you have just answered all my prayers."

***

True to Mrs. Walter's words, the work at the hospital was both difficult and unpleasant at times, but for the most part Cara loved it. She enjoyed making the sick children laugh, although her heart broke for those who would never get better. She had written her letter to her groom, a doctor named Colin Deane. In it, she described herself as mature, although Mrs. Walters had raised her eyebrows at that. She hadn't made her correct it though. She had also signed the letter Cara Donnelly. That way, if Senator Kavanagh did try to trace her, he wouldn't find Cara O'Donnell. That downtrodden girl with the domineering mother no longer existed. She was Cara Donnelly now, off on a new adventure, ready for anything. Wasn't she?

Click here to read more of The Maid: The 12 Days of Christmas Mail-Order Brides: Book 8

ABOUT THE AUTHOR

Piper G Huguley, named 2015 Debut Author of the Year by Romance Slam Jam and Breakout Author of the Year by AAMBC, is a two-time Golden Heart ®finalist and is the author of "Migrations of the Heart," a three-book series of historical romances set in the early 20th century featuring African American characters. Book #1 in the series, *A Virtuous Ruby*, won Best Historical of 2015 in the Swirl Awards. Book #3 in the series, *A Treasure of Gold*, was named by Romance Novels in Color as a Best Book of 2015, received 4 ½ stars from RT Magazine, and won an Emma Award for best historical romance in 2017.

Huguley is also the author of the "Home to Milford College" series. The series follows the building of a college from its founding in 1866. Book #1 in the series, *The Preacher's Promise* was named a top ten Historical Romance in Publisher's Weekly by the esteemed historical romance author, Beverly Jenkins and received Honorable Mention in the Writer's Digest Contest of Self-Published e-books in 2015.

Her series "Born to Win Men" starts with *A Champion's Heart* as Book #1. *A Champion's Heart* was named by Sarah MacLean of *The Washington Post* as a best romance novel selection for December 2016.

She blogs about the history behind her novels at http://piperhuguley.com. She lives in Atlanta, Georgia with her husband and son.